About the Author

A. P. W. Colgan was born in Perth, Western Australia. He studied history and literature at the University of Western Australia. After his studies, he travelled and has now settled in the south of France. He currently resides in the town of Antibes.

The Siren Sea

A. P. W. Colgan

The Siren Sea

Olympia Publishers
London

www.olympiapublishers.com
OLYMPIA PAPERBACK EDITION

Copyright © A. P. W. Colgan 2023

The right of A. P. W. Colgan to be identified as author of
this work has been asserted in accordance with sections 77 and 78 of
the Copyright, Designs and Patents Act 1988.

All Rights Reserved

No reproduction, copy or transmission of this publication
may be made without written permission.
No paragraph of this publication may be reproduced,
copied or transmitted save with the written permission of the publisher,
or in accordance with the provisions
of the Copyright Act 1956 (as amended).

Any person who commits any unauthorised act in relation to
this publication may be liable to criminal
prosecution and civil claims for damage.

A CIP catalogue record for this title is
available from the British Library.

ISBN: 978-1-80074-849-1

This is a work of fiction.
Names, characters, places and incidents originate from the writer's
imagination. Any resemblance to actual persons, living or dead, is
purely coincidental.

First Published in 2023

Olympia Publishers
Tallis House
2 Tallis Street
London
EC4Y 0AB

Printed in Great Britain

Dedication

For Gilbert VALE Rogues in Peace

Acknowledgements

I'd like to thank the following people for their contributions, editing and unyielding inspiration: Liss Lowery, Lidija Waldron, Elizabeth Richards, Alan Roberts and The Ménage Family.

CHAPTER ONE

A CARD GAME WITH FINNBAR

The Bar du Port in Antibes had every character you could imagine packed to its rafters. The clientele was a heady mix of rogues, sea captains, drunken sailors, fishermen, snakes, clowns, dealers, hustlers and entertainers. Even the town beggars would frequent it, usually when the affluent would drop by up from the Cap. Of course, these men and women were mostly, if not all, slightly unhinged weirdoes, all of them carrying a thousand stories. It was a rich tapestry squeezed into one little French coastal bar.

My friend felt right at home there. Naturally, it was where he told me to meet him. That was two months ago, so I wasn't sure I'd still find him there. I knew he could prop up any bar in the world. However, if I was being really honest, I wasn't sure if he'd still be alive.

That was Sebastian, or Seb as he preferred. He was big in stature and wild like the wind upon a winter sea. He was born on the tiny Indian Ocean island of Mauritius. He could sail a boat from the age of five and the sea salt ran through his veins. It had been a while since I'd seen him. I was looking forward to hearing his news, and as always, the stories I expected to hear would be epic – and mostly untrue.

Let me give you some background. We used to sail together. We started out working together and then became business partners. The first words he said to me as my captain were a shrieking, "Abandon ship!" He had a leaking hull, and the chaotic adventures began from there. We weren't friends at first, but we grew to tolerate each other as we travelled the globe by wind and sail. I guess we bonded through necessity. We delivered boats for people, mostly rich folk who had the money but not the prowess to navigate these fine vessels. We would spend time, wherever it might be, training new crew and showing them and the owners how to handle and maintain their beautiful yachts. For a brief time, we even took to boatbuilding. Seb and I, through years of squeezing out trust for each other, became bonded together by the sea. Sadly, as it turned out, when we expanded the business too fast, we went bust and lost everything.

That's when we started down our slippery path; we were thick as thieves, so, true to the expression, we decided to become thieves. We became smugglers. It started with small jobs first. The money was great and worth the risks. Then the jobs got bigger and the danger grew. We got into smuggling and soon enough smuggling got into us. We ran contra ban goods all over the world. From the Mediterranean Sea across the Pacific, Indian and Atlantic Oceans.

Our best run, before we got into trouble, was sailing a regular route from mainland Africa to the Island of Zanzibar. It was steady, profitable and felt like the closest thing to freedom I'd ever known. Sometimes we'd sail further south to Madagascar and visit all the little islands along the way and beyond. At first, we mainly shifted booze, undeclared hard liquor and, of course, from North Africa, hashish. Then it became a lot more hashish and then grew into moving counterfeit money and occasionally even guns. There was good money in those, but again, the danger would escalate. And so would the excitement. Our reputation for our daring grew, and so did our profits. Yet truly, I think we really loved it because we felt so free. It was uncomplicated in the wide-open sea.

Tricky situations were constant, and trouble was never far. But we were wild and carefree to the point of recklessness. When situations arose and the trouble grew too much, we always managed to slip our way out of it. Well, until we bribed the wrong guy and got pulled up in Tanzania. Doing time there made me rethink the business. But that was a long time ago now and, like I said, until then, the money was good and worth the risks.

Eventually, I gave it up, but Seb, on the other hand, never really left it. He worked in just about every country that skirted the Mediterranean. Now he had relocated to the south of France; luxury was more accommodating to him there and the money was better. My friend, the smuggler, had moved up in the world.

On top of his poor haggling skills, Seb was an accomplished bully, thanks to his size and temper. But he was one hell of a sailor, probably his only strength, because his negotiation skills left much to be desired: they usually ended in fights or us having to leg it. Yet his knowledge of the high seas and smuggling routes was immeasurable. He was a good captain and it made working with him almost pleasurable; you felt protected. I say almost pleasurable because, day-to-day, you wouldn't know which Seb would appear. One day he could be a firecracker of fun, the next consumed by the black dog of depression.

The trouble with being so wild is that it can sometimes come off as crazy. And Seb had a mad streak longer than a sunset. And to go with it, he had an explosive temper beyond control. Trip it, and a manic energy was unleashed. It was mainly triggered by the smallest of things. Like too much butter on his toast, or not enough tobacco in his pouch. If petty, manic behaviour had a smell, it would be his dirty, ugly sweat thrown in with a good measure of diesel, petrol and seawater.

Anyway, that was then – a long time ago – and this was now. A long walk up along a cobblestone road in the south of France was where I was now. It was going to be good to see him.

The Bar du Port shone with a warm glowing light. It was full of all the drunken revellers I mentioned. It smelt fishy and of old, damp wood. But walking into the bar, the sound was enlivening. After a long journey, I was ready for a drink. I'd been drifting through Europe for the last three months. Well, honestly for the last three years, but that's a story for another time. It was nice to stop. Dark rum and old beer stains soiled the old bar furniture. The wood beams above sank low and dripped condensed sweat. Pushing further through the bar, I grabbed a beer and looked around for him. His favourite spot in a bar was always the darkest and deepest corner, slouched on a barstool. I headed there and low and behold, there he was!

His eyes flashed on seeing me and after a double-take his face lit up.

"Alex! You've made it."

Falling off his bar stool, he bear-hugged me and wouldn't let go.

"You're alive." I played down my pleasure as I struggled free from his grip.

"My man! Have I got some news for you! You know that job I was telling you about?" he carried on excitedly.

"Yeah."

"Well, it fell through," he said through gritted teeth, yet still happy and smiling.

"Oh great, Sebastian. I've only come from halfway around the world for you to tell me this."

"Don't call me that! I've told you that a million times. Only my mother calls me that."

His news wasn't a real surprise to me, I was late coming over. I had missed the best weather for sailing and the summer was nearly over. The red skies were getting darker much sooner. It's as if he read my mind and found the silver lining.

"But don't worry, I've got something better. This is actually a great night to be arriving. We've got a card game on tonight. It's out the back, over there," said Seb, gesturing to a low, rickety door. It had a giant skull and crossbones painted on it and on the skull was scrawled, 'Privé'. Which even in my hopeless French I knew meant 'private'; that wasn't difficult. But the door itself didn't fill me with confidence.

"Let me guess, blackjack?" I rolled my eyes.

"Yeah, how'd you know?" he said with a big fake smile.

"Because you can only count up to twenty-one."

"Ha, funny! You haven't changed. Same old, smart Alex. Now that you're here, you'll be joining us."

"Seb! Really? You're terrible at gambling and you're a sore loser."

"Buddy, don't worry, it's not like in Zanzibar. No guns allowed." He smiled, slapping me hard on the back. "It'll be fine!"

I loved my old friend, but he really was a hopeless gambler. He loved the thrill more than the winning or losing. He had skin in the game, as the saying goes.

"Relax, Al, I know these guys, they're all soft touches and way smaller than me."

This was true, Seb towered over the patrons in the bar; he was large and strong, but, among other things, his main character flaw was poor judgement in picking fights. And incurable drunkenness, which, of course, caused the poor judgement.

"And remember," he carried on, "when I lift my left arm, two fingers raised—"

"Yes! Yes! I remember, turn the table up, throw some punches, grab some money and start running," I finished his sentence and sighed.

He hugged me. "I've missed you."

Seb was turning on the charm. I figured he was a little nostalgic for our adventures. I took it with a large pinch of salt, and we began to push through the crowd. At the door was a huge Arab doorman. I had actually asked him not to let us in. He looked at me with a slightly raised brow but regrettably waved us through. As we went through the door, Seb quickly whispered to me.

"Hey, by the way, old buddy. Can you spot me some money? Maybe a grand?" He paused and looked at me. "Or two?"

It struck me then as to why he was being so nice. Duh! I chose to ignore him and we carried on towards the table.

The back room was nothing short of a seedy den of iniquity. If the front bar was seedy, messy and sticky, this backroom, complete with another bar, of course, was its mother on dirty steroids.

We grabbed some drinks from a surly French barman along with his sneer, a prerequisite for securing a bar job in France. I looked over to the card table where a dishevelled-looking man stood up and pointed at Seb. He screamed in French, something along the lines of, "What the hell are you doing here?"

I quickly gathered that Seb was making himself at home. The angry Frenchman readied his fists. Seb swore under his breath.

"Oh, Christ, wait here a minute," he mumbled and moved towards the table. "Louis, I thought you were in Marseille?" He spoke in French, as did his friend, but I will give you a loose translation here:

"Ha! You would have liked that, no? No. I'm staying here to play. And I'll wait for my money. You'll pay me tonight, yes?"

"If I win, yes, of course, Louis," purred Seb. "If I don't, give me a week."

"Ahh," cried Louis, waving his hand in typical Gaul style. "Mon Dieu! You said that last week, Seb! You're a terrible liar. Terrible!"

"Yeah, I know, but don't worry. It's my lucky night tonight!" He beamed a huge smile and then he downed a large glass of rum.

The two men kissed cheeks, embraced and then Seb and I were permitted to sit and play at the table. It wasn't the outcome I was hoping for. Seb introduced me and I quickly whispered to him, "Uh, how many other people do you owe money to?"

Seb paused a moment, and I could see him doing mental arithmetic.

"In this room, just him. Don't worry, just a trifle of a debt."

I stared back at him with resigned disbelief, handing him a wad of cash.

"You better get us another job," I said sternly, "and soon. And it's ten per cent on top of this that I'm giving you."

He gave me a big, wet, rum-soaked kiss and we hunkered down.

"Get off me!" I said, wiping my cheek dry.

The table was long and the players were packed in like sardines. It was practically elbow to elbow. A card cheat's paradise. I sat opposite Seb. I squeezed in between a large Tunisian and an old man with a captain's hat on, complete with thick white beard and a pipe. The Tunisian was shouting at me in Arabic. It was completely lost on me. The Frenchman, Louis, was conducting the game. He held his hand out and I handed over my buy-in.

"You better not screw this up," I shouted over the buzzing table to Seb.

He smiled back, looking annoyingly smug.

"You parles Anglais?" came a deep crusty voice.

I turned to look at the voice next to me. It was the old sea captain.

"Yes, I do and if you look at my cards, I'll kill you," I joked. "I'm Alex."

"Aye, pleased to be making your acquaintance, young scallywag," was his reply.

"The name's Finnbar Roberts." He laughed and spoke in a thick Cornish accent. He looked every part the clichéd, salty dog. His naval jacket was tucked up under his thick neck and white-bearded chin. He carried on.

"I've been playing these here cards for donkeys and I have to say, I ain't never seen a worse cheat than that lad there."

His glass of whiskey in his thick crusty hands was pointed directly over at Seb.

"Don't listen to that old man, he's just bitter because I skinned him last game," snapped Seb.

"You cheated me!" cried Finnbar, puffing on a pipe.

"Well," I answered, "we're friends, but not what you would call the best of friends. We sailed together."

"Come on! Come on, Louis!" interrupted Seb. "Deal us in! Allez! Allez!"

The cards were quickly flung around to each player; it looked like a United Nations meeting for rogues. The noise in the room hushed a little as we began. The men at the table shifted around and became serious. Except for Finnbar, he sipped away on his whiskey and smiled to himself. He gave me a wink, which made me very uncomfortable. I couldn't wait to get out of there. But we played all night and the noise and screams got louder as the night rolled on. The drunker I got, the more I lost and prayed a little harder for lady luck to show.

The room was filled with smoke, I was nearly lost in it. Though I didn't mind as I smoked like a steam train myself. Fortunately, Seb was winning for a change. He was so pleased with himself and didn't hesitate to make it known to everyone. His pile of notes was growing so large that he was stuffing bills back into his pockets and buying rounds for everyone. The Tunisian sitting beside me, however, was not happy. He grew more menacing with each lost hand. He was losing heavier than me.

"He's cheat!" he spoke in broken English. "He is bad man, no good, no good!" He pointed his very large finger at Seb.

"I concur," agreed Finnbar, "He's a cheat."

Seb, with all the cockiness he could muster (which was considerable), blew a great, big kiss across the table to the Tunisian. The Tunisian lost his mind and grabbed a knife from his jacket.

"I kill you!" he screamed at Seb.

Louis (who was playing), the barman, and the small, skinny dealer jumped up and quickly disarmed him. They laughed and told the Tunisian to stop drinking. He begrudgingly complied and the cards were dealt again. The table was relatively calm again.

A few more hands were dealt, and I was just about out. The Tunisian was now finished and cleaned out. He looked across to Seb, who just couldn't help himself. He blew another kiss and mouthed, "I love you."

The Tunisian lost his head again and went absolutely crazy.

The small little smoke-filled place erupted. The big North African launched himself over the table and grabbed Seb's neck. Seb gave him a quick jabbing punch to get him off. He stood up and yelled at me.

"Alex! Alex! A little help, please?"

A big Russian, a drunken English sailor and a Frenchman at the table started going at each other. Fists and cards flew everywhere.

I ducked down as I was talking to Finnbar. We were deep in conversation. We jumped away from the table as I tried to ignore Seb's little scrap. It was proving more and more difficult to ignore as it grew in size.

"We aren't so much as friends, more business associates," I was telling Finnbar. "Well, former business partners."

"Ah, I see."

"Alex," yelled Seb again. "The left arm, the two fingers! Hello?"

Seb was taking a barrage of abuse for provoking the Tunisian again. He was now wrestling off several people at once. All the players at the table were now fighting. The barman had lost total control of the room. He was yelling and screaming and trying to kick people out of the door. He called for his doorman who burst in from the front bar.

"Screw this!" spoke Seb to himself.

And in unison, both he and the Tunisian threw up the table. The Tunisian wanted to get his hands on Seb. Seb wanted to get out of there with his money. The cards, money and drinks went flying. Glass was smashing everywhere. Everyone scrambled for the cash, snatching as notes and coins flew into the air like a green and gold volcano. The Tunisian and Seb were now face to face. They both threw punches and jumped on each other, wrestling. It was bedlam. I wasn't interested in joining the melee but inevitably got dragged in by another player. I took a punch to the stomach and fell over like a feather. Finnbar grabbed my assailant in my rescue but he, too, got battered. A rickety wooden chair cracked on his back, and he fell down hard on top of me.

Finbarr groaned in discomfort and looked at me with his crusty old smile. He smelt like a horrifying medley of old fish and whiskey.

"See, I told ye he was a terrible cheat," he said, groaning with a laugh.

We managed to lift each other up from the rabble. Broken glass was scattered across the floor. Finnbar had cut his hand and was bleeding. Seb was, again, fighting off numerous assailants while trying to keep a hold of his winnings. He was pulled down to the floor and grabbed at any of the money he could find. It was almighty chaos. I ventured over towards Seb to help his odds.

The dingy back doors had been thrown wide open. The large Arab doorman was throwing everyone out. He came thundering up to Seb and I with one arm on each of us. Picked up by the scruffs of our necks, he tossed us out the door. An angry Louis screamed in the doorway like he had when we'd first entered. He bellowed in French something that must've meant, "Don't come back!"

Seb protested and then yelled back. Louis and the doorman grabbed Seb and ripped the money from his jacket.

"Hey, that's mine!" yelled Seb, throwing a punch at Louis. The doorman quickly stopped him. The money from his jacket was torn out like a gutted fish and was now in the Frenchman's dirty hands.

The doors were slammed in our faces and our tails slunk firmly between our legs. Weary and drunk, we sat down on the pavement, broken and broke.

Ten seconds later, the doors flung open again and Finnbar was thrown out.

Seeing this, Seb rose from off the pavement and took another drunken lunge at the doorman. He was solidly knocked to the cobbled stones. He gave out a loud groan and began dusting himself off whilst lying horizontally. He turned to Finnbar, also flat out, and angrily said to him:

"This wouldn't have happened if you hadn't sounded your trap off!"

Finnbar couldn't get up and lay on the back street like a lump of old coal. His legs were rum and whiskey-infused jellies. But he lay on the ground, laughing in a drunken stupor.

"What's so funny, old man?"

I turned to Seb and spoke, "Seb, you're an idiot!"

"What? Want to say that again?" said Seb, lifting his head from the cold stones. He was so drunk and punched out, but he still managed to talk with steam coming out of his ears.

"Why is it every time you get on top of a game, you screw it up? I came here because you told me you had a job lined up. But you've got nothing. And now you've got less than nothing! AND you lost my money, as well!" I yelled.

Seb, looking bloodied and battered, tried to steady himself.

"I'm going to punch you in the face right now," he mumbled.

I shook my head, looking at the disgrace before me. I couldn't speak so I pulled out a bent cigarette. I tried to light it but realised I'd lost my lighter in the bar fight.

Annoyed and angry, I looked down on the cobblestone, desperately looking for matches or a light. All I saw was Finnbar, fast asleep. He was passed out and snoring like a pig. He was well and truly comatose. I reached down into his jacket pocket and finally found a lighter. I lit my cigarette, took a long drag and carried on.

"Great, and now we have to deal with this old mess."

"Who?" questioned Seb.

"Him! Father Christmas in a pirate costume," I screamed, pointing down at Finnbar.

"No, we don't, he does this all the time. Leave him there, come on let's go."

I was unwilling to leave this man for dead in the cold with probable alcohol poisoning. Much to my disgust, Seb was playing ignorant to the fact that this old man's impending death would quite possibly see us put in jail. My frustration with Seb's lack of conscience and responsibility was growing. I bickered with him until he agreed to help me carry Finnbar home.

"Jeez, all right, all right! Well, if you didn't find God, you've certainly grown a moral backbone and a whiney little voice!" said Seb, ridiculing me.

I felt so angry I couldn't speak. Seb, on the other hand, having had the last word, had calmed down and walked over to help me lift him up.

His pile of a body was stinking wet and a mess of bones and blubber. We were drunk but he was heavy and stank badly. His stomach was the size of a beer barrel and lifting his body was like heaving up a dead bull. His skin was tougher than leather. But we finally managed to lift his arms over our shoulders and began walking.

"Do you know where we're going?" I stopped and enquired.

"Yeah, to the port. Ole' Finnbar lives on his fishing boat as a matter of fact," said Seb.

"A fisherman, hey?" I said.

"Yeah, but he doesn't do much fishing," laughed Seb. "His

engine's been broke for about four months now. He's got no money to fix it, so he mainly sits on his boat getting drunk."

"Yeah, I gathered that," I replied.

"Yep, from sunup to sundown, yo ho ho and a bottle o' rum, and all that rubbish," laughed Seb.

We'd stumbled through the old ramparts and archways of Antibes to arrive at his boat. We were wet from the beer and spirits that had been thrown on us and the night was now cold. In the darkness, we barely made it aboard. The passed-out Finnbar nearly fell in, but we managed to grab him back from the shallow, inky abyss of the port.

Aboard his vessel, which had a strong stench of fish and petrol, Finnbar gave a small murmur of life. The old man was incoherent and mumbling like a broken-hearted fool.

"Aye! She was as pretty as a dish. Huh, wait, is a dish pretty? Oh, I tell ya, me boy, she was a petal and she left me," he ranted.

"Yeah, all right old-timer. Let's hit the hay," I said.

He fell onto the deck and made a loud thud.

"Urghhh," he groaned.

Seb did not look pleased staying on his stinking boat and went downstairs to sleep. I looked around the battered vessel for somewhere to rest my weary head. All I could find was a big mess of a fishing net taking up the deck space. That was as good as it was going to get. I was drunk so I didn't really care any more. Sinking into a pile of nets, I smelt a huge wave of old fish guts and diesel. It was pretty much what Finnbar smelt of, so I was getting acclimatised to it already. I did hold my nose and braced my stomach, nonetheless.

"She was a treasure!" Finnbar exclaimed and was carrying on in his sleep. "A treasure," he groaned.

Then, suddenly, he shot up from the deck and seemed

strangely more together than before. As if the bump on the deck had sobered him up. I was half-asleep when he rose. He came lunging at me and grabbed my jumper, squeezing it tightly.

"Hey, boy, young Alex, you want to see a treasure?"

His eyes had fire glowing from them, but I couldn't care less. I was ready to sleep.

"Yeah sure, Finn," I said nonchalantly, "I would love to see your treasure." I closed my eyes to sleep.

Finnbar carried on down to his cabin as I nodded off into the stinking net.

"Well, then, me boy," he returned, rousing me from sleep. He reached down into one of the hatches. "Argh! Where is it?" he said to himself.

He huffed below deck again and made one hell of a racket. Finally, he pulled out an old, salt-crusted, rusty iron box.

"I ain't pulled this here box out for near on three years now," he said, wheezing as he spoke. "And I ain't shown no one for near on five."

He tried to prise open the box but, in his excitement, he snapped an old tool and tripped.

He fell backwards onto another pile of fishing nets. Poor old Finnbar thumped his head and cut his hand again. The box fell with him, and he couldn't get up.

"Finn? Finnbar, you OK?" I said, tired and softly, not having the energy to get up.

I heard nothing back but the deafening racket of his snore. Good, he was alive. If I wasn't so drunk, it would've kept me up all night.

Thankfully, the fresh salty air and the sound of the sea took me back to my slumber without hesitation.

CHAPTER TWO

THE MAP

The sunlight wrecked a beautiful sleep. I dreamt of being in an igloo in the piercing cold, but I awoke to a splitting headache. The fishing net that was my blanket for the night was wet and the smell was worse now that I was hungover. I stuck an old cloth over my eyes. A seagull started screeching and picking pieces of fish guts off me and the net. It was time to rise. I slowly got up and saw the space where Finnbar had slept was now vacant.

Laughter was coming from down below. Seb and Finnbar were rolling around in stitches over coffee. I stood up and felt my head throbbing. A wave of old fish smell came over me. It was beyond brutal and got the better of me. I jumped to the side of the boat and vomited wretchedly over the edge.

The laughs from below grew louder as the two crusty pirates came up to watch.

"I thought you said your man was a sailor, Sebby?" laughed Finnbar. "A real son-of-a-gun, no?"

"Afraid not," said Seb, laughing also. "He can smuggle OK and he thinks he's pretty smart, but he's got no sea legs that's for sure."

Emptying my belly didn't sober me at all. In fact, it made me feel worse.

"Help!" I yelped. "Water!"

The two men laughed and Finnbar, now with a bandaged

hand, handed me a strong coffee with rum in it.

I tried to recollect the night's events as I rubbed the rancid sweat from my face.

"Here, there's plenty of water over there," said Seb, pointing to the port.

"Seb," I coughed. "You owe me money!"

"Yeah, yeah, I don't have it all on me," smiled Seb. "In fact, I've got bugger all as I was robbed if you recollect, so just rest your boots for now."

"I hate you! And hey, Finnbar, what was that box you were talking about?" I was trying to put my brain together.

"Hey?" Finnbar froze slightly. "I don't know what you're on about, me boy."

"Ah, yeah, something about an old treasure?" I was in a terrible haze.

"What?" Seb's face lit up. "Treasure?"

Finnbar's face turned ashen.

"Nope, I don't recall," he said, his voice trailing off. "Maybe a woman, I don't know."

"Yeah, you had some big old box you pulled out?" I replied. "And then you fell over."

"You mean that one?" said Seb, as he spotted the box laying under some nets.

Finbarr gave out a sigh and paused a moment.

"OK, OK! The game's up, I guess. Gents, I'm gonna now shows you somethin' that I ain't showed nobody in a fair old long, long time," grumbled Finnbar.

He crept down onto the net, his old bones creaking, and pulled up the old iron box. Seb gave me a puzzled glaze. He dragged the box over and slowly opened it with a key he had on the chain around his neck. It creaked with rust. We were suitably intrigued. Both Seb and I looked into it as deep as our necks could crane.

"Aye, bugger off, the two of ye," snapped Finnbar. "I'll shows ya, just steady on now."

He stood up and proudly announced the trove to his treasure.

"This here box is the secret to the greatest diamond heist ever seen on this here earth!" he proclaimed. "And it all vanished. Deep and dark into the mysterious sea."

"Let me see that!" exclaimed Seb as he jumped to look inside again.

Finnbar slapped him away. "Get out of it, ya scallywag!"

We sat down like children and watched Finbarr carefully take out each little artefact. He had old torn and tattered maps. There were newspaper clippings, all brown and worn. Polaroid photos and loads of keepsakes and trinkets. The trinkets were mostly seashells and colourful beaded necklaces. They didn't look like much.

"Where's the treasure then, Finn?" asked Seb, disappointed. "There's nothing in there except some old rubbish."

"Not here!" laughed Finnbar. "Like I told youse, it's been sunk into the sea far from here. I've been searching for it for donkey's years."

He gently handed some newspaper articles to us. The headlines were astounding.

'Diamonds Stolen Lost at Sea.'

'Big Heist Goes Missing.'

'Diamantes perdidos en el mar.'

Seb began to read bits of the article aloud.

"It was the greatest diamond robbery of modern times. The Costa Rican authorities, coast guard and government are still searching… It is estimated that thirty-seven million US dollars' worth of diamonds... were stolen from the state bank... And lost out to sea..."

"How did you get wind of this then?" I said.

"Well, I was there, boys, wasn't I?" Finnbar proclaimed proudly.

"What? No way!" both Seb and I let out.

"Aye, I was indeed," smiled Finnbar. "Costa Rica, 1966, me and the gang I was workin' for, we did it. Despicable men, the lot of them! They're all dead now, 'cept me but I ain't far off it. I just want to finds it before I leave this mortal earth."

Seb, naturally, exploded with excitement and illumination. We both asked Finnbar what seemed like a million questions.

"Is it still there?" said Seb.

"Where did you lose it?" I asked.

"Is it still there?" repeated Seb.

"Does anyone else know about this?"

"Is it still there?"

"We must go find it!"

"Yeah, is it still there?" said Seb. "We've got to go find it, Finn!"

"Aye, aye, AYE!" yelled Finnbar. "Cool your damned britches, the both of you! Just keep looking in there and ye'll find what ya need."

We both jumped to look down inside the box and cracked our heads together.

"Ye's a pair of knuckleheads," sighed Finnbar, as he pushed us aside again.

"How do you know it's still there, Finn?" I said, rubbing my skull. "It was 1966 you said—"

"Because I buried it!" interrupted Finnbar with a huff. "It wasn't lost to sea at all. Well, some of it was but I took it and buried it in the jungles. And I've this to show youse."

From the old box, he pulled out a tiny piece of a map. It had been torn and ripped from a larger one. He shoved the little piece right into our faces. It had scribbled pencil on it, marking out coordinates of longitude and latitude. And, of course, an 'X' to mark the spot of the buried treasure.

"Here!" he cried with excitement. "It's the coordinates I buried the treasure at, right here!" He jammed his finger into the ripped piece.

Seb and I were totally gobsmacked.

"You're a genius, Finn!" said Seb, almost in dreamland. "Al, can you believe it? We've found our Shangri La!"

"We've?" laughed Finnbar. "We? Yes, that's right. I'm no fool you know, boys. There's no we in this here equation. Just I, aye."

"Well, presumably you've told us about your little treasure so we can help you find it, right?" I chimed in.

"Well, you presumed correct, Master Alex. But we've not spoken about the split as to when AND if we find it, now, have we?"

"OK, this is good," smiled Seb. "Negotiations are underway."

"Well, now, don't get too far ahead of yourself either, Sebby. Firstly, and most importantly, what we needs to do is figure out how we are going to get over there and by that, we need to be pooling our resources in doing so."

"Ah, what do you mean? We're just going to get on a plane and fly, right?" I said.

"Yeah, let's go tomorrow," agreed Seb.

"Wait, wait, wait! We can't just be getting up and going up on a plane to find these treasures," stated Finnbar.

"And why not?" questioned Seb. "We can be like treasure hunters. I've always wanted to get into that."

"Because I can't be putting my name anywhere near that place!" exclaimed Finnbar. "I did time for that! And it would turn out just like the last time I went there. Men got shot there and *died*! It was a bloodbath. And I have a name there. I've a bad reputation and I've been banned from ever returning. A black mark, boys. A black mark!" His voice was full of foreboding.

"Oh!" said Seb stupidly.

"But I tell ya, boys, it was one hell of a piece of daring," smiled Finnbar. "The brazen audacity, the bravery, the sheer ferocity! Fortune does indeed favour the brave!" he exclaimed.

"Well, why don't Seb and I just go?" I reasoned.

"I may be old but like I said, I'm no fool," snapped Finnbar sternly. "And I've been doing jobs long before you two were off your mothers' bosoms. I know what I'm doing, and I know you two wretches are as trustworthy as foxes in a hen house."

"So, how else... hot air balloon?" I said sarcastically.

Finnbar looked around the port and raised his arms to show us what was around us.

"Boat, my boys. We go by boat!" he exclaimed.

"Urgh," I groaned.

"If this here is to be my last attempt as I grow with the sands of time, then I should like it to be done under the mast. Call me a foolish old romantic but those are my terms, boys."

Finnbar shut the lid down hard onto his box and beamed a broad smile. Seb and I quickly agreed and gave out a cheer.

"Boat it is, then," we sang.

The last attempt, I wondered, and put the question to him, "How many times have you tried to get this treasure back before, Finn?"

"Just a few," said Finnbar looking a little sheepish. "And we failed each time. I tell ya! It ain't gonna be easy, nor easy sailing. But we should all come back in one piece... not like the last time."

"Oh, that's reassuring," I said as my hangover kicked in again as my fragile head sunk.

"And besides, my bones ain't getting younger. They grow more brittle by the day – and my rheumatism. That's why I came to the south of France, for the sunshine and vitamins. Time is not on my side any more, gentlemen. This is my last charge."

"Well, can you still navigate? And sail?" said Seb.

"Jesus wept!" scoffed Finnbar. "Of course, I can. You never lose that. But if truth be told, I've been waiting for a couple of likely young ruffians like yourselves to give me one last hand."

"Well, then," I said. "We thought it was our lucky day, but it turns out it's yours!"

"Yes, indeed. Look at what the rat dragged in!" Finnbar bellowed with laughter.

"Hmm, yeah, that's not funny," I mumbled.

"So, what sort of boat do you want to use, then?" said Seb, getting down to the task. "How can we get a boat then, hey?"

There was no question of not pursuing the treasure. This was the moment I'd been waiting for. We really didn't have anything left to lose, other than our lives. But through the years, we had gained enough experience to handle high-pressure situations and know when to stay and fight, or when to run like scared chickens. The main issue we had was the logistics. How on earth were we going to do it?

Excitingly, we were the only ones on this planet that knew of this beautiful little secret, as far as I was aware. If it had been there for over thirty years, a few weeks of planning would not go astray. So, time was on our side. It was too good to be true. The thought of hundreds and hundreds of diamonds, stuffed in hessian bags, pulled up from a seabed floor and now buried deep under a sandy floor in a jungle. It made me mad with hope and wonder. Seb, of course, wanted to leave right away but we had to address our logistics problem first, for which there were a few solutions.

"Well, you know the motor on my boat is shot to pieces," said Finnbar, carrying on the conversation. "You know, Seb, I've been tryin' to get you to bloody well fix it for donkeys, haven't I?"

"Yeah, you've never got any money!" snapped Seb. "And the parts are miles away from here. Anyway, this little stinkpot wouldn't do it. We have to go across the pond," Seb continued. "We don't have the range and even if we did, the cost in fuel alone, Christ, we're a bit screwed. Unless you all want to row?"

"*Row*? Good lord, not in my condition. Come on, boys, we have to sail. Think! We can all sail, so we can save on fuel."

We were building up a lot of hope and planning on a paper-thin story. Realistically, there was a slight chance that the diamonds were still there. Yes, the clippings had confirmed the diamonds were never found. But near on forty years of erosion, who knew if other foragers or wannabe pirates could have found it years ago and not said a word? But the hard truth was that in our circumstances, it was a risk worth taking. Seb was jobless and broke, and I was next to broke and jobless.

Maybe coming across Finbarr was a sign that the universe was looking after us. Or perhaps it really showed how desperate we were. Either way, it was a real low point. To know what we were potentially sitting on and not have the means to go find it.

I kept answering my own questions in my head. Yes, to travel two weeks across the Atlantic Ocean to look for old, buried treasure from forty years ago was sketchy. But like I said, we had nothing else to do and we lived for this stuff. So here it was, handed to us on a plate by Finnbar. Bless you, Finn!

Seb, meanwhile, was pacing around on deck. The cogs inside his mind were slowly clicking into gear. He grew more and more animated with each step as he thought about the problem.

"Wait!" yelled Seb. "I've got it. I've found a boat we could use."

"Well, spit it out then," I begged.

"Yes, Master Sebastiona! Bravo! Please enlighten us, if you will?"

"It's over there." He pointed towards the outer walls of the port. "She's perfect. Old, a bit crusty, beautiful lines, a sturdy helm, big keel that glides through the ocean, holds itself in a stormy sea, at times she's bloody tough to handle but she's a beauty. AND she's banged up so we also couldn't be luckier, it's so good!"

"She sounds like me," laughed Finnbar.

"Banged up?" I was wary.

"Yeah, like, she's chained up," Seb continued. "The owner didn't pay the taxes on the boat, so customs locked her up."

"Customs! That's not good. How do you know all this?" I asked.

"I did some work on her at the start of the year. But it's all locked down. Everyone got laid off. You must know it, Finn? It's that classic old schooner. It's famous!" finished Seb with excitement.

"Oh, it's famous all right. *The Queen of Ionia*," nodded Finnbar. "Aye, she's a real beauty all right."

"Exactly! She's our treasure catcher!" proclaimed Seb.

"But she's famous for all the wrong reasons," Finnbar continued. "Do you know who the owner is?"

"Yeah, of course. I worked on it," said Seb.

"This doesn't sound good," I mumbled.

"He's Italian Mafia!" cried Finnbar. "His family owns half of Naples. He's not paid his taxes on the boat because he doesn't pay any taxes. In fact, he shot the taxman! That's why he's in jail."

"He's an Italian gangster, big deal!" Seb brushed off our alarm. "Don't worry, I've heard stories."

"Well, then, are you sure you want to be taking his boat?" asked Finnbar.

"Yeah, I'm with Finn," I chipped in. "This doesn't sound like a solid plan. I think you've finally lost the plot."

"He's in jail! In bloody Rome somewhere," Seb exclaimed. "That's why it's perfect. It's exactly why it's perfect. No one will suspect it's us, they will go chasing Mr Italian Big Shot and his minions."

"OK, moving on. How shall we be commandeering this vessel?" enquired Finnbar. "It will be crawling with customs officers, up and down and all over."

"I don't think so," Seb declared. "It's the weekend, tomorrow is Sunday. We won't see an official or a uniform. It's France!"

"This be true," agreed Finnbar. "It's crazy but it might actually work."

"So," Seb continued his plan, "in the dead of night, we jump aboard, and tomorrow, we buy plenty of supplies: food, fuel, medical supplies, everything we can think of," said Seb with glee.

"I think we need to create a diversion."

"Hmm, fair point, Alex," said Finnbar. "The harbour master won't be in but there'll be someone knocking around."

"On the other side of the port," I continued. "Smoke and mirrors."

"Mm, I like it!" said Finnbar. "I can get the young lads from the Bar du Port. They'll be happy to help. They're always looking to cause trouble, paid or not."

"OK then, great. We have a plan!" yelled Seb in triumph.

"So, tomorrow night, then!" I said. "And what about the split?"

"Well, we go thirds, right?" said Seb. "It was my plan after all."

"Huh!" laughed Finnbar. "Let's be getting the boat first with our lives intact and then we can begin our parlay."

"Sounds OK to me," I said.

"Strong winds, and perhaps a storm, might blow up from the east in a day or so. I'd go sooner if we could," added Finn, warily looking out to sea.

"Good, then the easterly winds will carry us faster away from here," said Seb. "Once we are out of French waters, we can relax a little. We will still have Spain to deal with but after we are out in the open and out of Europe, we are good. Nothing but the big blue sea!"

We all cheered. It was a decent enough plan, even if it was cobbled together. I loved the excitement. Seb had a steady hand and was always pragmatic and ready for adventure.

I truly believed he should have been born in another time. All he seemed to dream about was finding gold and treasure and sailing off to a paradise island. He had a pirate's soul. I suppose all three of us did.

I remember several years back; Seb and I sailed through

Madagascar. On the high cliff tops was an old grave of some French pirate from the 1700s. He died of typhoid trying to carve out his own Republic of Utopia. On the old windswept gravestone was the standard RIP carved in it. But underneath in large font, it read: ROGUES IN PEACE. We've adopted his philosophy ever since.

"Alex, you need to get provisions this afternoon!" said Seb, whipping into a panic.

"Yes, I'm aware of that," I replied.

"I'll load up the extra fuel and go see my doctor," said Seb. "I don't know what medicine is on board there."

"I'll be fine with this," said Finnbar, popping the cork to a bottle of port. "It's medicinal, after all."

The church bells of Antibes sang out. It had struck midday. And as the chimes rang out, our rogue pack was made. The next night, we would set sail, a ragbag team of buccaneers. We were going to find Finn's lost treasure, buried under a beach half a world away. It was a long shot, but hell, we were going to enjoy searching for it. These were the days worth living for. I felt a joy I hadn't felt for a long time. We were lucky to have met Finnbar, but if I had to, I would singlehandedly find his diamonds and run away to a far-off island and never come back. I know Seb felt the same. Maybe it was our destiny.

But then I looked over at Finn getting drunk and I had second thoughts.

"Finn, maybe you should slow down, we'll be leaving tomorrow night," I pleaded.

"Nonsense, Mr Alex!" replied Finnbar, now sozzled and grinning merrily. "Now's the time to celebrate!"

"Hmm, I'm always dubious of a victory party before a victory, Finn."

"Just wait until you see them! These diamonds and rubies are so shiny they glisten with a madness. You just look at them by the sea in the midday sun and they blind you, my boy!"

"Are you sure they'll still be there?" I queried again.

"Oh, she'll be there! I haven't forgotten and I never will." His eyes grew distant as he looked out to sea. "Salvation awaits, Mr Alex! Salvation awaits!"

His voice trailed off into a song as he went down into his cabin. I began to leave. I smiled and raced to the shops. His madness was catching on.

CHAPTER THREE

THE QUEEN OF IONIA

Seb and I walked side by side in the dead of night. We walked slowly towards the port, pushing two large shopping trollies that rattled annoyingly. One was full of fuel and tools, the other packed tightly with food and medicine. The smell of petrol, fresh fruit and veg and adventure was heady.

But the sky was dark and the night cold. We walked in silence. Except for the stupid trolley wheels. We also carried adrenaline and fear. The trollies banged through the cold wind which picked up at each step. Seb knew the way to our vessel. We tried hopelessly to be inconspicuous and normal, but we looked like two down-and-out bums, though that was probably good as no one would pay us any attention.

We were meeting Finnbar on the outer wall of the port, just by the boat. Seb kept some tools hidden underneath some blankets; we were ready to break whatever locks and chains were holding her to the dockside. And just like the moon that was starting to poke through the black clouds, it was now our time to shine.

As we drew closer to the boat, from over by the rubbish bins, a torch flashed two clicks.

"Who goes there?" Finnbar's salty old voice whispered.

"Hurry up, Finn, get out of there and quit it with your bloody flashlight," cried Seb in a whisper-shout.

"All right, all right," said Finnbar, ducking out from behind the bins.

He smiled proudly and marched out, feeling all resplendent in a once-bright yellow fishing coverall and boots. On top, he wore a crusty yellow wet-weather jacket and rubber hat. The great Shackleton would have recruited him for an Arctic adventure.

He hobbled over with his rucksack and hallowed iron box. His hobbling guilted me into helping and we carried on.

"Keep up, Finn," whispered Seb.

Then, on the dockside, under the bright moon, momentarily free from clouds, was the mighty schooner. She was magnificent! Her two masts were glowing in the moonlight. Her rigging whistled in the winds. What a mighty soul of oak and craft. She was glorious. I stood and stared and lost myself in the moment of laying my eyes upon her.

"Ah, now that there is a truly fine vessel wouldn't ya say, Mr Alex?"

We both stood and took it in. The sheer majestic beauty was a moment to behold.

"Will you guys hurry the hell up?" yelled Seb angrily. "I don't want to be looking at this boat from the hilltops of Grasse prison!"

"Aye, aye, captain," said Finnbar.

Seb crept onto the boat which was side-to on the dock. He snuck towards the aft and began lowering the passerelle. We all began to work as quietly as we could, loading up our provisions and fuel tanks onto the aft deck.

"And call your guy, Finn, it's nearly time," whispered Seb.

I loaded our last box of tin food and handed the bolt cutters to Seb. Finnbar pulled out an old mobile phone from his jacket and made a call. Seb jumped down to the helm and opened the wheel box with a screwdriver and bolt cutters. He hurriedly looked around for a key to start the engine. Fortunately, he knew where the old captain stashed the spare keys. His hand and arm peered into a wooden crevice and out came his hand, holding a key, a big smile on his face. Next, we began to cut the chains, the steel snapping slowly with each twist. Now just two lines held us to the dock. We would take these in when we were ready to move with stealth.

BOOM!

A large explosion erupted from the other side of the port. It looked to be a boat catching fire. Smoke rippled into the night sky. This was Finnbar's diversion. He was looking over at the distant flames with a cheeky, satisfied smile. His happiness creased his furrow.

"Well, I won't be needing this old junk no longer." He threw his phone into the shallow water of the port.

"Finn, get in here," whispered Seb. "Mind the helm while I get to the engine room, I need to get the fuel down there."

The flames bellowed like a war dance. Police cars and fire engines shone and flashed their sirens in the distance. We were heading for safety in our getaway. We had some time. Seb primed the engine below and gave a yell to fire them up. Finnbar turned the key and, with his squinty eyes sparkling, gave a thumbs-up as the engine came to life.

I proceeded to drop the lines and we slowly crept out of the Port of Antibes. It was a brief stay, but lively. Thanks for the memories, Antibes. If this trip brings me fortune, I shall never forget you.

The motor puttered away as Finnbar took the helm. Seb rose from below and kept a lookout, as did I. We dared not run any electrics until we were out of harm's way. No lights – mast, port or starboard – were we to switch on. It was a stealth mission and we stayed in the shadows as close as we could.

Once out of the harbour, the black abyss took hold. We pushed away further from the lights of the land. We settled into the cradle of darkness. It felt vast, yet comforting, as we broke for freedom. There was no going back for Finn and Seb. They looked back to their home with nostalgia. The door was closing but a new one on the horizon was beginning to open. The three of us grew fixated with what lay ahead. There was exhilaration and fear in one.

Finnbar sat in the cockpit. He was beaming as he took in the old boat's beauty and there was plenty of it to behold. The smell of oak and varnish lapping through the sea was beautiful.

Seb and I snuck downstairs to check other supplies inside and familiarise ourselves with the boat's layout.

"I've got to go to the captain's cabin. I need to get out the charts," said Seb.

Down below, we could feel the wind picking up. It was the easterly Finnbar had spoken about. The mast rigging began to whistle harder. We were down below but it was dark. We still weren't running with our generator for fear of being spotted. Seb shone his flashlight towards the captain's cabin. It was at the furthest end. He tried the door softly, but it was locked. He began to lift the handle, and lift it some more, but still nothing.

"Just bash it in," I suggested.

Seb started hitting the door hard with his broad shoulder. But every time he hit the jammed door, his rejection made him angrier. Taking a deep breath, he bashed it as hard as he could and the door flew open.

BANG! CLATTER! THUD!

He snapped the lock from the old wood which splintered. All I could hear was a heavy thud and a painful yell coming from him.

With my torch, I looked down at Seb, who was now out cold. Flashing my torch around, I saw an object flying towards me. I took a thump to my arm but dodged the full attack, whatever it was.

I leapt back to view my assailant. Standing over Seb was a woman in a rage, looming with a frying pan.

Her stare was piercing as she screamed and yelled like a mad harpy. She lunged at me again.

"Wait, wait! Don't hit me!"

"Who the hell are you?" she screamed.

I didn't know what to say as I swayed and dodged her swings. She reached for a little battery light by her bed which lit up the cabin. I dropped my flashlight and, at the same time, dropped my jaw.

It's precious moments like this one when you think you're about to get beaten up but instead get hit by Cupid's arrow. Seb's attacker was the most beautiful woman I'd ever laid eyes upon. She was fierce, wild and ready to strike again. Her arms were flexed high, ready to strike.

"OK, let me explain," I yelped frantically. "Could you please just put the pan down... please?"

"NO WAY!" she bellowed. "What are you doing here?" She paused and heard the engines running. "Hang on, are we moving? ARE YOU MESSING?"

And with that realisation, she screamed and launched her frying pan at me again. Her hair was a wild, curly, golden brown. She was scary but so beautiful. She hit me again, so I had to wrestle the pan off her. I failed dismally as I kept staring at her ferocious, wolf-grey eyes. She whacked me again across the head and I fell to the floor.

My head was facing down to the floor. All I heard was Seb groaning too. He lifted his sore head up but just as quick the woman jumped on him and whacked the frying pan across his face again. She looked at him again and screamed.

"SEB? What are you doing here?"

"Hang on wait, you know this guy?" I asked nervously, getting up.

Seb was bleeding from his head and looking pretty groggy. His hands were held up in defence.

"Don't hit me!" he yelled.

The woman looked more and more like a wild warrior princess. She grabbed his arms from around his face and yelled, "Seb! What are you doing here?"

Seb looked up dazzled and winched in pain.

"Charlie? Is that you?" he murmured.

"Yeah," she said, slightly calmer now that she knew her enemy. "What the hell are you doing here?"

Seb groaned.

"Ah, what am I doing here? What are you doing here, more like it? I thought you all left. You shouldn't be here!"

"Am I missing something here?"

The fact they knew each other helped me relax and less fearful about getting hit by her pan again.

"I had nowhere to stay," she said. "I've been hiding in the captain's cabin for the last month." She paused and listened to the motor. "And where the hell do you think you're going?" She stood up looking out the porthole. "What have you done, Seb?"

I felt it was my time to introduce myself.

"Hi, I'm Alex and yes, we've commandeered this vessel."

She didn't speak to me but gave me a filthy death stare.

"Ah, you're welcome to join us?" I mumbled.

I was pretty sure, right then and there, that I had dropped my dignity and self-worth on the cabin floor.

"You're crazy!" she yelled at Seb. "What the hell do you think you're doing? I've got a job interview tomorrow."

Seb was still coming to his senses and the fact that his friend was aboard our stolen vessel.

"Hang on, you're living here? Why?"

"Yes! I'm trying to save money."

"Well, worse places to live," I reasoned, trying but failing to lighten the mood.

Again, Charlie looked me up and down with utter contempt.

"Ah, this is my friend Alex," said Seb, getting up from the floor.

At that point, Finnbar poked his crusty head down the cabin.

"What's with all the commotion? Is everything OK down there?"

"It's fine!" yelled Seb and I in unison.

"No, it's not fine!" screamed Charlie.

"Aye, we've a lass onboard. Oh, Lord, 'allo missy, the name's Finnbar," he said, smiling.

Charlie had a look of pure rage. She flared her nostrils to the size of two small volcanoes.

"Get me off!" she yelled. "NOW!"

Finnbar was calm, clear and smiling away.

"Now, that's all good and well but we can't be just dropping you off somewhere here willy-nilly. We've commandeered this here vessel for a little adventure. So, we'd be kindly asking you to sail with us out of these here French waters… or else we'd be having a small, delicate problem."

"Oh my God," shrieked Charlie. "I'm calling the coast guard!"

She rushed to move as Seb stopped her.

"No, no, no! Charlie, let me explain!" he begged.

Seb followed Charlie up to the deck and held her gently, begging and negotiating with her.

"Charlie, please! Yes, we will drop you off! Anywhere you want but once we get out of French waters. You know we've stolen this boat so we can't do it now. We are going on an adventure."

"Don't touch me! You boys are idiots!"

"Yes, that may be true, but we didn't expect anyone to be on board, especially not you! Please, Charlie."

"Please what?" she replied, still furious.

"Well, I really don't want to have to tie you up and gag you!"

"YOU WOULDN'T DARE!" Charlie was totally incensed and started to freak out.

"No, I wouldn't. But these guys might," Seb said, looking at me.

Again, she looked me up and down and flicked her wild, gorgeous hair into my face. I was scared of her but was so captivated by her high, Athenian cheekbones. I was a stunned mullet and couldn't say a word. I just nodded like an idiot.

"Look, it's your choice," pleaded Seb again. "Stay with us until we get to Spain, but don't try anything funny."

Charlie tried to calm down.

Finnbar looked at her and stupidly said, "Can you cook? We do need a chef on board."

Charlie had another total meltdown. It was understandable.

"Sorry, was just asking," said Finnbar, somewhat taken back.

"OK," said Seb, taking a spare line from the deck.

Finnbar and I looked at each other and knew this wasn't good. Seb quickly took the rope and wrapped it around her waist like a lasso. Charlie kicked and screamed but with Seb's size, he was able to overcome her efforts.

"That's the spirit," cried out Finnbar, making Charlie go even more crazy.

"You'll pay for this!" she screamed. "Kidnapping! Stolen boat! You'll never get away with this! If the coast guard doesn't get you, the mafia will!"

"Yeah, we'll see," said Seb, ever so calmly. "We'll drop you off in Spain, don't worry. But sorry, you won't be getting that job. Alex, go down to the cabin and take her phone."

Charlie slumped down angrily into the cockpit, all tied and bound. But as she moved, she grabbed with her bound hands a wooden gaffe and swung it towards Seb.

WHACK!

It was another crack to his head, and he hit the deck again. I took the weapon off Charlie, which was much easier to do now that she was tied up. Seb lay on the teak deck but was still conscious.

"Are you OK? How you feeling?" I asked, looking down.

"I feel Zen," was Seb's dry reply. "Very Zen!"

Charlie sat down in the cockpit, quiet but satisfied.

I went back down to her cabin and grabbed her phone. With my flashlight, I could make out some tools by her bed and a couple of knives amongst some make-up. And above her bed was a Liverpool football scarf. Well, her being from Liverpool would explain her fiery temper and ferocious ways. But it was understandable, we did ruin her job interview.

Back up on the deck, Seb went off forward, holding his head. We began unfurling the sails right open. It was time to get back to sailing. The wind was full, and we needed to pick up our speed. Finnbar smiled out to sea. He held a firm grip on the helm.

"So, what are you doing stowing away on here like a refugee?" spoke Finnbar. "Trouble with the law? Man troubles?

Saving up to run away?" He laughed.

Unsurprisingly, she didn't answer.

As we slowly pushed further out to sea, the darkness overwhelmed us. Our beautiful old schooner glided through the black abyss. Just the moonlight shimmered and sparkled on the now-deep water we were above. Further and further we floated, out to the beyond. I'd like to say we were on a wing and a prayer but none of us were the praying type. I had given up on God a long time ago. So, we just set sail and let the wind take us forth.

Despite the wind picking up, the sea was quite still. It would take half a day or so before the whitecaps sprayed onto us from the seas and the swell of waves would blight us. For now, we were away and needed to get as far away as we could.

I continued with Seb, giving a hand up forward with the rigging and sails. We set aloft the mainsail to gain some speed. I looked back to the cockpit to see Finnbar in his element. He beamed a broad smile, looking to the wind and proudly steering this grand ship he now had in his possession. I was happy for him. In fact, I was over the moon.

So far, we had done what we had set out to do and we weren't in jail. It was progress from the last adventure Seb and I had had. But we had gained an unwanted new crew member. A reluctant one, which didn't bode well, but nonetheless, we had one more for our motley crew. I turned to look at Charlie, trying not to be noticed. She stared out into the darkness. Her blue, ocean eyes were piercing. I had to admit, having her on board was a welcome respite from the unhinged cretins I had set out on this perilous journey with. I welcomed the beautiful distraction.

CHAPTER FOUR

THE PILLARS OF HERCULES

The art of piracy is nothing sensational. Shamefully over-romanticised, when the reality is much dirtier. But it was a truly wonderful feeling to carry out such work on the Mediterranean Sea. For here, in these ancient waters, piracy is as old as Homer's *Iliad*. It made me think of a story I remembered from my school days. When the great Roman emperor Julius Caesar was a mere officer in the legion, he was kidnapped by a band of pirates in the Greek islands. The pirates, detecting his social rank, proceeded to hold him for ransom. The future emperor, shocked at the vulgarity displayed by these men, tried to culture his captors by reciting poetry to them. They were not impressed and quickly displayed their contempt.

As history tells us, the ransom was granted and Julius went back to Rome to continue his life of splendour. The pirates, of course, continued menacing the merchants of the Med. That was until Julius became emperor and he saw it fit to stamp out this malarkey. He returned to the Greek island of his captors and had them all strung up to trees and cut to bloody ribbons, telling his generals to let them stew in their own blood.

Well, I would still choose this gambit. They, and we, were too proud and full of desire. And we had a great love for adventure and chasing riches. I was just thankful the Romans didn't rule the waves any more because we'd all be stewing in our own blood by now.

The sun was breaking through the morning. We had sailed all through the night. The wind took us as far as it would carry us. Over the red sunrise, we brushed through the ocean at a lulling pace. All through the night, we had clambered all over the boat, getting a feel for this beautiful old schooner. I watched the sunrise with my legs dangling over the bowsprit. The deep blue water was vast and immeasurable.

I looked back to see Finnbar looking at the sea, his hands still firmly on the helm. He looked wondrously happy. Seb was running around maintaining the now-fully hoisted sails and checking in on the engine room and charts. Charlie was next to Finnbar in the cockpit, still tied up but a lot calmer. She looked pensive, staring out to sea. It was a glorious morning. We had no sight of land now, the constant gusts of wind on our backs which carried us further and further out to sea. France was long behind us, and at that moment, I felt a small amount of freedom that I hadn't felt in a long time. But there was plenty more work to be done.

"We're going to have to be changing this girl's name, you know?" called out Finnbar to us both. "We need to stay under the radar, gents."

"I thought that was bad luck," returned Seb, yelling from among the masts and sails.

"Aye, 'tis true Sebo, my boy, but in these here circumstances, we've no choice," returned Finnbar.

"Any suggestions?" I said.

"Yeah, *The Mother Load*," cried Seb with a mocking smile.

"How about *You've Got No Hope and You Should be in Jail*!" yelled Charlie.

"Yeah, nice one, Charlie," laughed Finnbar. "Maybe a bit too long."

"No, I've got it: *The Siren Sea*!" exclaimed Finnbar with glowing pride. "That's what we are going to call her. And that's where we'll find her," he announced.

"I like it," I said. "It's got a romantic ring to it. *The Siren Sea*! Nice, Finn!"

So, now we had our ship for our unruly adventure. And between maintaining our sails, Seb and I chipped away all morning at the old wood lettering. The Queen of Ionia was to be banished into history! With some old paint, we hastily painted on *The Siren Sea*. It took all of our efforts, but it was a labour of love. Exhausted from having spent all morning in the sun, we fell below to the galley and began to cook and crack our first beer in celebration. It was a mighty pop, opening our first bottle. The foam and beer spurted out and we drank it down, fast and merry. It was the tastiest beer I'd ever had.

The galley was sparse, with a lot of healthy food of Charlie's which didn't particularly interest us. We brought out our supplies, made a small feast and stayed our course. Finnbar opened his first bottle of rum and began to sing louder and louder as the bottle emptied. The fresh salt air washed over the boat as we glided onwards. The sails stretched in the gentle winds. Finnbar was half-drunk now, but he held steady on the helm. Our spirits were high. This beautiful schooner swam and cut through the ocean like a giant swordfish, its bowsprit proud and true.

"So, Charlie, we're off to seek some treasure!" exclaimed Finnbar, sitting down next to her.

"Oh, here we go! And the name is Charlotte and at the first moment I get, I shall be jumping off-board," she said tersely with her broad Scouse accent.

"Uh, Finn, I don't think you should be telling her what we

are doing," I said.

"Ah, that's fine by me, more treasure for us. Just don't be alarmed if we keep you tied and even muzzle you up," he said, tongue in cheek. "You can't be tellin' no one of our little 'venture you little Scouse scallywag."

Charlie was infuriated as Finnbar continued to gulp down his bottle with merriment. He chuckled at Charlie's contempt.

We brought up the sandwiches, a mix of cheese, pickles, ham and plenty more bottles of beer. The day was growing more glorious by the hour. It was, of course, helped by the illumination of the alcohol. And hour-by-hour, more beer sank down our bellies. I offered Charlie a sandwich, but she refused.

"Are you sure you don't want something?" I asked kindly.

"No," she flatly replied.

"You might starve to death," I said smiling.

"I'm vegetarian!" she snapped back.

"Oh!" was my reply as I took the ham out of her sandwich and placed it next to her. At least she was talking to me now.

Seb, in one of his manically happy moods, then jumped up with a spark of an idea.

"Hey, Charlie, do they still have those clay pigeons aboard?" he said.

"Seb, you are a first-class fool! You've just stolen a mafia boat and now you want to make a scene by shooting guns off the back of the boat?" returned Charlie.

"I don't see anyone," replied Seb. "I'll take that as a yes!" he said excitedly and jumped down below deck again.

"Heavy drinkers in small vessels," laughed Finnbar.

Seb returned with his wild-eyed smile and began setting up the clay pigeon sling contraption. I held the shot pellets and double-barrelled rifle. Charlie looked with disdain and carried on with her venom.

"You guys are the biggest idiots I have ever encountered," she snarled. "I can't actually believe you've gotten this far."

"It's only those who are broke that will help you repair," retorted Finnbar.

"What?" murmured Charlie. "And where the hell are you going to find this so-called treasure anyway?" she snapped.

"We are heading west until the butter melts," beamed Finnbar. "Here, mind the helm for me, dear," said Finnbar in caring tones.

"Oh yeah, what with?" she said, still tied up.

"Well, now, I guess you're a part of this motley bunch, young Charlotte," he smiled.

Finnbar untied her and proceeded to swan off towards the stern which sat closely behind the cockpit. I was a little worried seeing Charlie now free, but I figured she wouldn't be so stubborn as to jump into the water and swim. It would be to her peril.

Seb was starting to test the sling for the clay pigeons. We three men, as stupid as we were, had just stolen a boat and began an expedition across the Atlantic to find some long-lost diamonds. But we had only one thought: to shoot stuff.

"PULL," yelled Seb.

The first clay pigeon went flying and a large boom came thundering from the old shotgun.

"Damn, missed," said a now drunk and merry Seb. "PULL," he said again, as he clipped one.

Cheers rang out among us as we rotated the rifle. Charlie continued her tirade as she gripped the helm.

"See, Charlie, this is fun!" smiled Seb.

"For a start, your captain can't sail very well because he's absolutely drunk," she ranted. "He's self-opinionated, chauvinistic and thinks he knows where he's going and can't even hold a course straight. And I don't know where the hell this boat is going but you're finding some treasure? Yeah, right!"

"Ah, yeah," I turned to say. "And Seb's the captain by the way."

"Even worse!" she laughed. "And you," she continued fierily, "a little smart-arse nerd who hardly speaks and doesn't know a boats' arse from its head."

"It's called a bow, not the head," I replied, as the boys laughed, continuing to shoot into the sea.

"You little boys are delusional," she carried on. "And you think the best way is to steal an old, slow gentleman's yacht – which, by the way, you guys are not going to get away with – you're doomed!"

We all looked at Charlie, stunned for words. Yes, it was true we were clueless putting our trust in an old drunk. It was a leap of faith from a drunken night. And now we had an irate hostage. But still, I never knew a happy one.

You're clearly upset by this, my dear," said Finnbar. "Here, have a drink," he offered, slinging his rum bottle at her. She took it and threw it overboard, to Finnbar's dismay.

So, of course, we did what any genuine pirate would do, we grabbed another bottle from below and carried on drinking and shooting clay pigeons until they ran out. We sailed a smooth enough course, further towards our destination, with Charlie as our reluctant helmswomen and hostage. We all watched the sun slowly set to the west, where our dreams lay ahead. As we sobered up, except for Finnbar who took over the helm, we sat in quiet reflection, just the breeze pushing our sails gently forward. It was a fantastic afternoon and evening as the sun set in the brilliant red sky.

But as night fell, I heard the soft, quiet sobs of Charlie breaking through the silence. The excitement turned to fragility for the rest of the long night and the next couple of days. We had to get her off the boat as soon as we could.

However, we were quite unnerved by Charlie's words, and we got spooked. Spanish authorities and coast guards most certainly would have been notified of the stolen vessel. The three of us gathered in a huddle and whispered amongst ourselves. Finnbar announced our thoughts to Charlie.

"Dear girl, we've had a brief discussion and our unanimous decision is not to go to shore in Spain."

Charlie looked at us in disgust. "You liars!" she cried out. "Who do you think you're talking to? How dare you hold me prisoner!"

Her protests fell on deaf ears as we continued sailing our course. We had enough supplies, so we carried on towards Gibraltar. It was upsetting but we insisted on being out of harm's way and into safer waters before we would release her.

So, with the wind picking up, ensuring us a few more knots to run with, we were entering another night. The sun had set in another glorious pink and red sky. Charlie was forlorn with sadness and anger. She didn't say a word. It was best to let her be. I took the helm as the stars began to shine. The next day or so, we would find the Straits of Gibraltar. We all felt uneasy due to it being a heavy shipping route. We would remain calm and vigilant as we sailed past the mighty and ancient rock of Gibraltar, the gateway from the Mediterranean to the Atlantic.

The ancient Greeks called it The Pillars of Hercules. The north pillar was Gibraltar, and the southern pillar was the mountainous peak in Morocco which the Arabs called Jebel Musa. Beyond those pillars lay the mystical city of Atlantis. From the Greeks to the Phoenicians, giant sea monsters roamed and instilled fear into sailors. Tales of terror continued for centuries, and the renaissance scribes coined it onto their maps.

'NON PLUS ULTRA', which translated from Latin to: 'NOTHING FURTHER BEYOND'.

It served as a great warning to merchants and sailors.

I did a job there briefly shipping hash from Morocco to Spain, particularly Gibraltar. There's not even twenty miles between them. The Kif from the Rif, they called it. In Morocco, the Rif Mountains were where acres upon acres of marijuana were grown for the world's demand. It was north of the Atlas Mountains where they grew even more. I didn't like the job much as there were too many wide boys and gangsters from London and Essex in the business. That meant too many guns for my liking. But I enjoyed visiting the rock and reading the history.

The ancient stories proclaimed that Hercules had smashed through the rocks that joined Africa to Europe. He created the Strait that led the Med to the Atlantic. Ulysses, as written in Dante's *Inferno*, sailed past the Pillars in order to gain knowledge of the unknown. But after the Americas were discovered, the Spanish coined a new motto for their propaganda machine.

'MULTI PERTRANSIBUNT ET AUGEBITUR,' which translated to: 'MANY WILL PASS THROUGH AND KNOWLEDGE WILL BE GREATER'.

For them, knowledge was finding where to sail so they could steal the gold that the Incas and Aztecs had buried in South America. In fact, they even stole the motto from Sir Francis Bacon. He had an unfinished script *Novum Organum*. I never read it but I realised we've been stealing since humans came out of caves. That, and, I also concluded, the postmodern world existed before we knew it. My last thought was that the Spanish were really good at stealing stuff. They were proper thieves, nearly as deplorable as the English.

So, as the winds blew in from the Atlantic Ocean, we sailed past the mighty Rock of Gibraltar. Trepidation filled the air.

We looked alert and pensive, searching for patrol boats or coastguards which might have been tipped off of our presence. Charlie peered out to the coast and cursed us once again. It was a dilemma not of our making. We weren't to know of our stowaway, nor she of our intentions. But our next port of call would be outside European waters. It would give us some respite and for Charlie, her freedom.

CHAPTER FIVE

GYPSY BLOOD

Entering the great Atlantic Ocean lifted our spirits. It was deep in size and breadth. I knew it was steeped in deep mysteries. And many souls had been long lost and forgotten in its waters. But looking down at its dark depths didn't give me the shivers, it gave me a jolt of electricity and I felt so alive and so small amidst the biggest element on the planet.

And so, we sailed on towards the Azores. We sailed for over four days. One thousand, one hundred and ten miles we covered. This leg of the journey was relatively smooth. In fact, the last couple of days of sailing had let us drift slowly into a mental and physical state of excitement, even Charlie, who was happy and closer to be leaving us. I had seen we were quickly surpassing our daily rations for booze and food. The situation was becoming precarious, but we knew land was not much further ahead. Yet another night we would sail through, drinking and being merry, and another drunken dawn would break with glorious pink skies. And so the pattern continued.

The last day before we hit the Azores, the morning sun had burnt away the early morning clouds. We were not to be deviated off our quest. Seb sat in the cockpit, steering. He and I were steely determined to find this God-forsaken treasure. It became an obsession. The others I cared not much for, just the rupture of riches. Charlie was asleep, wrapped up in a blanket, although still mesmerising and resplendent in her slumber with the sun reflecting off her golden curls. It created a dazzling, almost angelic glow. Finnbar came up from below deck, yawning and stretching with the obligatory bottle of rum in his hand. In the other, he held an expensive-looking pipe which he had found in a guest cabin, carved from ash. He happily exchanged his old one, throwing it into the ancient sea.

"Ah, rum and tobacco, the great elixir to friendship!" he rejoiced.

"Speaking of which, we're running pretty low on both," I said.

"That's OK," said Seb. "We've gotten through the straights of Gibraltar and we load up again in the Azores." He peered out to the ocean. "And I need to get another few blocks of hashish. We are all running low. But fear not, we'll be there by midday."

Sebastian, being born on an island, carried the same disposition as all other islanders around the world. He loved nothing more than to swim, eat fish and smoke that mysterious plant of great healing remedies, marijuana. Like the Rastafarians, he held the plant sacred and sought spiritual awakening from it. It was his solace and anchor. Often, it was his crutch to lean on, for better or for worse.

We were within sight of the Azores and were heading to the island of Sao Miguel; the large town of Ribeira Grande on its north-east side was our destination for now. It was the closest island we could get to; Seb's spiritual supply of hashish had ended in the last day's sail and he was beginning to get restless and anxious. Finn, too, had squeezed the boat dry of liquor. He resorted to drinking old Italian cooking wine, which he moaned about to no end. The great illusion of utopia had begun to leak.

As the salty air blew, we came to the island. I could only

describe it as remorselessly windswept. It was a lanky promontory of granite, filled with greenery. It peeked out from a vast ocean. Its habitation had spawned from old trading routes of spices and slaves, the bedrock of every empire. This old settlement was Portuguese and was now a sullen, sunburnt and hard-bitten tourist destination.

The Portuguese were, for a time, the greatest navigators and explorers the world had seen. Vasco de Gama was their greatest. He sailed here and carried on south, along the west coast of Africa. He was the first European to arrive in India via the Cape of Good Hope in South Africa. I thought our four and a half days sailing from Gibraltar were hard at times. This guy sailed three hundred consecutive days once and covered twenty-four thousand miles. The hardships brought harsh measures, from one hundred and seventy men, only fifty-four returned home from India. And what was the biggest illness and cause of death might you ask? A scourge that had taken many men upon the high and low seas, far and wide. Scurvy.

A pirate's greatest fear on the high seas was this, even above not finding treasure. And so, harking back to my school days, reading historic tales of valour and damnation, I decided it was a good time to buy oranges, lemons and limes when we came to port.

As we drew nearer to our port of call, our apprehension grew. Seb stood up and began.

"Now, everyone, we drop anchor a few miles outside the port, just around the bay. We don't need to make a commotion or cause a scene," Seb spoke with firm determination. "We are free, but we don't want to alert the authorities to our happiness."

He surveyed the coastline, binoculars glued to his eyes.

Drawing nearer to the port, the tension grew. We were to

drop our dinghy which was sat tied down to the ship's forward deck. We had tested its engine over the last few days and it was in decent working order. The atmosphere was positive, yet unnerving. Charlie was gathering her things. She looked happy to be leaving our gang of desperados. I was a little sad, to be honest. Despite the berating lectures, I enjoyed her company. Seb turned to Charlie.

"Charlie, have you got any money?"

Charlie rolled her eyes and was ready to give him a serve.

"No." She refrained from letting go as she now felt a sense of relief, she was going to be free.

"Please, I'll pay you back next summer back in France, you know I'm good for it!" he begged with binoculars glued to his eyes.

It was true that we were broke. I had thrown my last few hundred dollars into the pot, as had Seb and Finnbar. But it amounted to very little. We had literally begged, borrowed and stolen to get this far. It just wasn't enough, clearly, for this jolly ship of desperate fools.

"Well, that's a laugh. You'll be lucky if you're still alive," she mocked.

"Please." Seb tried to sadden his eyes, getting down on his knees, as if begging for forgiveness.

"OK! Get up would you? You're embarrassing yourself," Charlie agreed, taking pity on us as she continued. "But try to stay alive, would you? Seb, despite being the worst work colleague and friend I have ever encountered, and despite you kidnapping me, I actually do care about you!"

It was the sweetest thing I had heard from her and it gave Seb a little quiver of emotion.

"Thanks, Charlie, I'll do my best." He quickly gave a cheeky smile and added, "And thanks for not calling the coast guard, must still be love, hey?"

"Oh, you're such an arse! I want it back. I'm saving up and I need this money back, OK?" she huffed as she sat in the dinghy, ready to go.

The landing party consisted of Finnbar, Charlie and myself. Seb was to stay at anchor onboard the vessel. We set off in haste.

"We'll be mighty sad to see you go, Charlie," said Finnbar. "Normally I like my tea strong and my woman weak, but for you, I'll make an exception."

"Thanks, Finn," she said, rolling her eyes. "I hope you find what you're looking for."

"So do I, my dear, so do I," he replied.

"What are you saving up for?" I asked Charlie. "A house? A marriage? A dog?"

"None of those, you moron," she said. "I'm saving up for a café."

"Oh, nice," I replied.

"Oh, and I hope with tea and scones," smiled Finnbar.

Charlie smiled and we carried on. Entering the harbour, we navigated through numerous fishing boats. Our tender spluttered and passed the harbour walls. We headed to the hustle of the port.

We drew nearer to a foul-smelling quay. It was full of old, rundown-looking fishing boats, meshed together with old ropes and squawking seagulls. There was a lively fish market on the dock. Finnbar looked at the seagulls with annoyance. He was trying to wave them away as they squawked at his fishy old jacket.

"Go on and bugger off you vermin." He shooed them away.

We docked and Charlie and I helped the old salty dog out of the dinghy. We looked for fixed objects to take our bearing and noticed Finnbar, who, upon touching land, had become wide-eyed, heading towards street vendors and market traders. He asked the price of fish and was flabbergasted by the prices.

"OK, Master Alex, get yourself into those stores and give me a call when you need some extra hands."

I looked at Finnbar, perplexed, as he headed straight into a port tavern. He yelled on his way, "Be sure to get plenty of port. Any port in a storm, that's what we say!"

I headed straight to the local supermarket on the dock. Seeing Charlie next to me about to wander off, I turned to her.

"Are you going to be OK?" I said.

"I'll be just fine," she replied, but with slight hesitation.

"Well, you can always join us," I said, with delusional hope. THUD!

Just as I finished talking, I felt a blow straight into my back and fell to the floor. A man running had fallen on top of me. I looked up from the ground as he lay on top of me, face to face. I groaned in pain. The woman he was with screamed and helped him up. He had fear and desperation in his eyes. Just as quickly as he had hit me, he was up again and running. Charlie helped me up as five men came bashing into us again. They were yelling and screaming, obviously the man's pursuers.

"Well, this place ain't what it used to be," said Finnbar, yelling, bemused from the other side of the street. I dusted myself off and we carried on.

The shop was right by us as we said our goodbyes to Charlie.

"Goodbye now, Charlotte. Good luck, my dear," said Finnbar, bowing and holding her hand.

"See you, Charlie," I waved.

"Bye, guys," she said, giving us a wave back. "Thanks for the lift. And thanks for letting me go… in the Atlantic Ocean," she said sarcastically.

Finnbar left for the tavern and I entered the shop as we left Charlie, who shifted through the market, backpack on her shoulders. She looked back and I gave her another wave from the shop doorway. I was a little sad, I had to admit. It would have been nice to have met her under different circumstances, like seeing her in a pub or bar, somewhere normal. Not kidnapping her on a stolen boat. I entered the shop, thinking of another one of life's rich ironies…

After stocking up, I grabbed Finnbar, who was now drunk again from his quick tavern jaunt. We went back to the dinghy. All we had to do now was wait for a local hash dealer, which I'd promised Seb I would get for him for our next leg. I stood around the port waiting like a third wheel. Finnbar was sitting in the dinghy, singing. In these ports, however, it didn't take long for trouble to come by and, soon enough, a tall African man approached me. He hissed and asked what I needed. As I was negotiating, the same man who had bashed into me, ran past me and jumped into our dinghy. The woman he was with followed suit and fell in after him. Finnbar was in the dingy and got the fright of his life.

"What in the Jesus hell is going on here?" he yelled.

"Please, you have to hide me," said the voice. He spoke English but his accent was Spanish, I think.

"There are people after me, bad people! Please!"

Finnbar, being Finnbar, agreed and wrapped a tarpaulin that was in the dinghy over the two of them. He nestled the shopping on top of them. The five assailants quickly rushed through the crowd, stopping at me. The African man quickly ran away before we closed the deal. Seb was not going to be happy. One of the men, large and angry, came up to me and yelled; he was brandishing a machete.

"Where is the man?" he snarled.

I gave a look of shock and shrugged.

"I think he went that way," I spoke, pointing to the other side of the dock.

They quickly darted a look towards Finnbar, who tried to look nonchalant and less drunk than usual. The angry men headed off. Finnbar lifted the covers.

"Righto, you two! What's the bloody meaning of this?"

"Sir, please, sir, these people are bad men, you've got to get us away from here. They want to kill us!" the Spaniard whispered.

"OK, all right, wait a minute here." Finnbar turned to me and spoke. "Mister Alex, it appears we have a quandary."

"Oh great, another!"

"What say we take them with us?" he enquired.

"Ahhh, no."

"Please, sir!" cried the desperate Spaniard, looking dishevelled and covered in bright tattoos from head to toe.

In this line of work, it was highly problematic to have both a moral code and a conscience. Unfortunately for me, I did, though I wish I didn't.

"Yep, OK whatever. Just hide them! OK, Finn?" I yelled. "Jeez, this will really screw up our rations, but I'll let YOU explain that to Seb."

"Aye, it's done," said Finnbar proudly.

"Come on, hurry up, then," I yelled to Finnbar.

We started the engine. The boat was fully loaded up. We dropped our lines, started to leave the dock and took off, fast. The Spaniard and woman were wrestling under the covers to make themselves comfortable. As they poked their heads up, a yell from the dock rang out. It was one of the assailants, still lurking around. He yelled to the other side of the dock, screaming to his gang.

But the screams that were heard throughout the port caused a huge commotion. Even Charlie returned and came over through the market traders. She looked out to us still in the harbour and asked if we were OK, yelling at us from the dock. The pursuer looked at her and quickly grabbed her. He continued his screaming over the port to his gang. It was nothing short of a disaster. I turned to Finnbar who was looking out to sea, steering the little two-stroke engine. He was oblivious.

"Finn!" I screamed. "Finn! Turn around, we've got a problem here!"

I could see Charlie yelling and trying to break away from the man's grip. She was elbowing him, to no avail. As we came to the dock, I could see the other members of the gang running back over. It was not looking good – a race to get to her first before they got to us was on.

"Hold tight, Alex, boy!" yelled Finnbar, now seeing what was happening.

We raced back and frantically swung portside to the dock. Without thinking, I jumped onto the dock and lunged at the guy holding Charlie. Surprisingly, I knocked him to the ground, perpetual motion, I guess. Charlie broke free and Finnbar yelled at her to get in.

The rest of the attackers were fast coming up the dock and I quickly followed, jumping into our little rubber boat. All hell was breaking loose as the men arrived, pushing through and knocking over the market traders. Our Spanish guests were screaming back at the men. A rusty machete came flying in our direction. It landed next to us in the water with a splash. We sped away as fast as our little, now-overloaded boat could go.

"What on earth was that?" cried Finnbar, as he looked back at the commotion.

By now, the Spanish man was on his knees, kissing Finnbar's hand and thanking him profusely. He gave a big yell to his attackers again and cursed them with something horrible in Spanish. It was a lively supply run. I looked at Charlie. She looked thankful for me saving her, but she also had her familiar flared nostrils of rage. She couldn't quite believe she was back with her kidnappers. I thought it best not to discuss what had just happened. I didn't want to make things any worse. Best to get back on board and get the hell away from this little rock of weirdness in the middle of nowhere.

"Welcome back, Charlie! We missed you," smiled Finnbar.

Charlie was not amused.

The Spaniard and his companion were now out from underneath the covers. They smiled and held each other tight. The Spaniard was so excited, he almost fell in as we headed back around the bay, our dinghy bouncing upon the waves.

"What are your names?" I asked. "Where are you from? And *why* are you running away?"

The Spaniard stood up proudly and began, "I am Alonzo Fernando Alberto Vladimir Nesto, the Gypsy Prince of Catalonia. And this is the love of my life, Mariposa, the queen of my heart!"

"Gee, that's a little dramatic," said Charlie, shaking her head in horrified awe.

Mariposa smiled deep and fondly at Alonzo. She, too, had illuminating tattoos of flowers, hearts and mythical creatures.

"Mariposa, Spanish for butterfly," smiled Finnbar, "I love it! May your love blossom, amigo. It can be blind but beautiful! I'm Finnbar, by the way. And this here is Mister Alex and our dear

Charlie, returned to us!"

Charlie had a death stare and I, too, was dreading the return to our boat. We had supplies but now twice the crew and no special supplies for Seb. He was going to hit the roof. I used to love the sea. It was uncomplicated for me, just the big blue space. But now, this was going to be an interesting trip, if it wasn't already.

We approached the newly christened *The Siren Sea* and came alongside, tying up and loading our new crew aboard. Seb came over and looked down into the dinghy in shock at our ever-expanding crew list.

"What the hell is this?"

"Captain Sebastian," Finnbar quickly injected. "Yes, indeed. Look what we have here. Apologies, dear captain, but sometimes the best-laid plans can be laid bare. And we saved these good people here from great peril."

"And what are you doing back?" exclaimed Seb, looking at Charlie.

"Don't ask," Charlie snapped, "Thanks to the SS Knucklehead!"

Our new shipmate Alonzo was smiling broadly. He came aboard with his Mariposa and quickly introduced himself.

"Hello captain, I am Alonzo Fernando Alberto Vladimir Nesto, the gypsy prince of Catalonia!"

Seb observed his new crew and tried to stay calm.
"Spanish?" he said.

"I'm afraid so," I replied solemnly.

"Spanish," he said again mumbling to himself.

Seb held the same opinion as I did towards the Spanish. We had nothing hugely against them but from experience, we thought they were the biggest thieves on the planet. And they'd steal from you whilst smiling in your face. I suppose we were being a little prejudiced.

Seb turned to Finnbar and looked for an explanation. Finnbar came to the rescue of our new crew and defended them with glowing pride.

"It turns out these two lovely souls were on the run; armed men were trying to take them hostage…"

Seb interjected, "Well, I'm not surprised, he's annoying me already! Alonzo Fernando blah, blah, blah. And what's with the Vladimir?"

"Captain," Alonzo carried on, "I am truly thankful for our rescue. It would be a deep honour if you could please take us to wherever you're travelling to, we shall be very, very most thankful."

Seb ignored them and turned to me.

"Alex, lift the anchor and let's get out of here."

I left them all to get acquainted and hastened towards the bow. However, as I started pulling up anchor, I could see in the distance two, small, rubber dinghies heading our way.

"Ahhh Seb, looks like we've got company. Our Spanish friends' friends," he said.

Seb turned towards their direction, peering out with his binoculars.

"Well, keep lifting the anchor, will ya!" he yelled.

He stared daggers at Finnbar and then quickly jumped down below. As the dinghies were approaching, he came back on deck with the large shotgun. Thankfully, he had found a new box of shells. I kept lifting the anchor as I watched them approach. Finnbar and Charlie had managed to get the dinghy back on board and we were just about ready to haul out.

"Hey, Spanish guy!" said Seb. "You and your girl need to

hide down below. We've got your friends wanting to come over for dinner."

"What?"

Alonzo peaked over the side and saw them approaching. He grabbed Mariposa and they quickly dived down below. Once the anchor was up, we set off under motor and sail. I ran to the stern with Finnbar and Charlie. We stood firmly behind Seb. Finnbar and I grabbed boat hooks, each ready for trouble. The two small dinghies approached. Seb held firm, gave the helm to Finnbar, and blasted two shots towards the attacking crew. He gave a wild yell, cussing and swearing. A spray of pellets punctured one of the rubber boats. It burst with a bang and the men on board panicked. The other dinghy fired a couple of shots which we all saw coming. We ducked and Seb fired back. They were torn between pursuing us and helping their fellow bandits. Another blast from Seb was enough to send them packing back to port.

"That should do it," said Seb.

We breathed a sigh of relief and headed out into the wide ocean once more. We left the Azores behind and, with double the crew now onboard, Seb and I tried to go over our rations and watch keeps, planning for the next ten days. We would have to do a lot of fishing, which was no chore, but the whole situation was dicey. Seb was not happy and what I was about to tell him next would make it worse.

"Have you got my stuff?" enquired Seb.

"No," I said bluntly, "I had a guy on the dock but then everything went crazy."

"I'm not hearing this!" said Seb. He kept repeating out loud as a way of trying to process the disappointment.

"Sorry," I said, in a poor attempt to console him. "You'll be OK!"

Seb, in an apparent effort to distract his temper, made himself busy and mumbled his disappointment. We carried on, of course, and the Atlantic Ocean now engulfed us. There was still plenty of work ahead. Even Charlie mucked in. She seemed resigned with her lot and just got on with it. We all carried on preparing the vessel for the trip ahead.

And just like a fish out of water, Alonzo tried overly hard to make himself useful. He managed to get caught up in the lines while trimming the sails with me. I could hear Finnbar laughing at him in the background. He got flustered and pulled out a small knife from his belt. The line holding him took a lightning-quick slash from his knife, cutting it instantly. The small forward jib sail went flapping in the air.

"What are you doing?" yelled Seb, from the cockpit.

"So sorry, captain, forgive me please," replied Alonzo, bright red from his now subdued anger.

Seb came lunging up past us to save the sail. He grabbed it and screamed at Alonzo.

"What the hell! You do that again, Spaniard, I'll throw you overboard!" he yelled.

I went to help Seb. The two of us spent time reigning in the sail and making new lines fast. As the wind picked up, we spoke:

"Whatever you do, Al," whispered Seb, "do NOT mention anything about the treasure, all right?"

"As if," I replied. "Not only is he Spanish but he's a gypsy too! And have you seen his tattoos?"

"Yeah, I've seen them, and I don't like it," he replied. "Knives and hearts! Just stay on your guard, OK?"

We spent some time tying another line to the sail's end and sent her flapping into the wind again. As we headed back, our new crewmembers were sitting in the cockpit with Finnbar. The salty old dog was holding court and I could just hear him tell our new guests of our secret and – not to be discussed – quest.

"I think it might be too late," I said, turning to Seb.

"Oh, great!"

Finnbar sat there telling his tale like an old king embellishing a won battle from long ago. Alonzo was naturally intrigued, as everyone was of Finnbar's wild story. It was wearing thin on me. Alonzo was translating to Mariposa, who didn't speak English, but she smiled back at Alonzo with excitement, talking back animatedly and laughing. Alonzo, seeing us arrive, saw it as a grand moment to stand forth and announce his arrival.

"Captain Finnbar!" announced Alonzo.

"He's not the captain," interrupted Seb.

"Excuse me, captain, but if I may—"

"Not really," Seb interrupted again.

"OK, OK, capitán, please," Alonzo pleaded, "may we begin?"

Alonzo then stood on the wooden benches to make himself taller and ripped off his buttoned shirt which bared two tattooed swords on his chest. A cheer came out from Mariposa and he began his animated, snake-charm speech.

"Good captain and his kind friends and crew members, I grandly wish to deeply thank you for saving me, the great Alonzo Fernando Alberto Vladimir—"

"Yeah, yeah, we've heard all that!" interrupted Seb, rudely. "And what's with the Vladimir?"

"I concur, captain, I'd be fascinated to hear this," added Finnbar.

"For God's sake, let him speak," shouted Charlie.

"Thank you, madam," said Alonzo politely. "Well, if you must know my father, Alonzo Fernando Senior was the Gypsy

King of Catalonia, and he had a wonderful love of Dracula."

Finnbar gave out a snort as Alonzo continued.

"So hence and so forth that great name was added to my fine lineage of gypsy blood," Alonzo declared.

"Oh, great," I sighed. "A blood-sucking Spanish gypsy."

"Uh, Dracula wasn't a gypsy," spoke up Finnbar.

"Yes, he was, Finnbar," argued Alonzo. "His home was Transylvania, Romania, the spiritual home to the great Roma gypsy tribe."

"Ahhh, well I'll be buggered."

"Right, I've had enough of this," said Seb, raising his voice and grabbing Alonzo by his ripped shirt.

"Listen here!" Seb continued. "You need to pay to be here on this ship, OK? And about this imaginary treasure that you might've heard of. This here guy is off his rocker," Seb yelled, pointing at Finnbar.

Alonzo jumped down in fear as Mariposa ran to comfort him.

"It is quite all right, capitán, I shall pay you handsomely for our passage," scoffed Alonzo. "I've no need for your petty treasure, for I have my own."

He turned to Mariposa and spoke to her in Spanish, sweet tones of love.

"Darling, please," he said pulling away from her loving hands and addressing his audience again. "If you would be so kind…"

Mariposa so delicately pulled out, from under her flowing garments, stacks and stacks of neatly wrapped euros. Hundreds and hundreds of euro notes were dropped onto the floor in the thousands. Alonzo gently grabbed a pile off the floor and threw them down again to great dramatic effect.

"Capitán," he declared, "take me to your destination!"

Finnbar nearly choked, slugging down a new bottle of whiskey, fresh from my supply run.

"Good Lord!" he coughed. "See here, Seb, I knew there was something good about this lad."

Seb and I looked down at the pile in disbelief.

"Where did you get this?" said Seb. "Anything to do with those people chasing you by any chance?"

"Yes," said Alonzo with great pride. "I stole it from them!"

"Huh!" I gave out a laugh. "I knew it!"

"Well, what a surprise, you'll fit right in here," laughed Charlie, looking too, with disbelief. She sighed, returning to her cynicism.

"But it was mine. I stole it back from the men who stole it from me. It was my money!" raged Alonzo.

"Bravo, Alonzo, bravo!" cheered Finnbar.

"So, Spaniard, how did you get that?" said Seb, who suddenly took a shine to his new crewman.

"My old bosses," replied Alonzo. "The men who were chasing me. You see, I was in the circus, their circus. We travelled all over the continent. Mainly around Spain, my homeland, of course, and Portugal for many, many years. And I was their greatest performer!"

"The circus?" smiled Seb. "Sounds about right."

"Yep, does explain all the theatrics."

"So, what did you do?" asked Charlie.

Alonzo smiled and looked at his dear Mariposa. She smiled back and, again, from underneath her flowing dress, she slowly pulled out a set of knives, tied and bound in leather. She handed them to Alonzo who proceeded to pull them out.

"Woah!" yelled Seb, who started to clench his fists. "What do you think—"

"No, no, no, capitán, please," he calmly interjected, and before the words had left his mouth, he took a knife in his left hand and flung it towards the mast.

WOOSH!

The blade flew past like a mighty hawk and stuck firmly into the mast. The knife jammed dead centre into the old oak. Finnbar gave out a mighty cheer.

"You see?" carried on Alonzo. "I am the greatest knife thrower the world has ever seen. That's why they call me The Great Alonzo Nesto, the Gypsy Prince of Catalonia, knife-thrower extraordinaire!"

"Bravo! Alonzo, bravo!" repeated Finnbar. "Do it again!"

Mariposa laughed with joy, looking fondly at her man. Alonzo blew her a kiss and continued.

"You see, in the end, I was not paid by these terrible people and the boss, the big boss, tried to take my Mariposa away from me!" Alonzo then flew into a mini fit of anger. "And I will not have this injustice brought upon me! Nor will the queen of my heart be stolen from me," he raged. "As my dear grandmother would say: 'For when you are given, eat! And when you are beaten, run away!'"

And with that, he again threw another blade, as quick as the eye could see. The knife sat embedded right above the first blade, exactly in the centre of the trunk again.

"Well!" Finnbar said, greatly impressed. "That's some story, all right. Welcome aboard, guys!"

"Yeah, OK, sure, great story, Spaniard," said Seb. "I'm sure you've got plenty more. And mate, thanks for the money," he added, slapping him firmly on his back.

Seb bent down and grabbed a wad of notes.

"But there is no way in hell you are keeping those blades on you while you're on here," he said firmly.

"OK, capitán, I agree," relented Alonzo humbly. "You and

your crew have saved me from great mortal danger and so the least I can do is take away anyone's temptation."

"Hey?" questioned Seb. "Mine or yours?"

"No, no. Please, capitán, please let Mariposa and I cook you a beautiful Spanish meal."

"Not Spanish," I interjected.

"Make it Gypsy. Gypsy will do just fine," Seb said, giving Alonzo another big smack of affection on the back.

So that evening, there we all were a ragged band of gypsies, pirates, runaways and thieves. We sat down to a wonderful banquet. Even Charlie relaxed and was smiling and laughing. She was happy to have some female company despite the language barrier. We sailed on and had lost sight of land long before we realised and were now in the midst of the ocean.

That night was a moment of pure bliss. The sails were bursting with the fine wind in them. The sun set in a magical, illuminated pink and orange sky. And the company was fine and ample. If we could've stayed like that for an eternity, I would have been truly happy.

And as the night drew on, the drunker and merrier we became. It turned out the sweet Mariposa was the circus tarot card reader. That night, she taught Charlie how to read the cards in the little Spanish Charlie knew. We all shared a story or two or three to great laughter. They were all quite similar tales of daring and desperation. Despite our different backgrounds and cultures, we were all the same – vagabonds and chancers that would never stop running or chasing. And to cap off a really entertaining night, Alonzo's knives, of course, came out, and we all had turns at hitting the mast.

CHAPTER SIX

A BANK ROBBER'S OLD TALE

We had sailed for four days since leaving the Azores. Our grand vessel, the fine and mighty *Siren Sea* bobbed along at a leisurely speed. We caught fish along the way, mighty tuna that fought hard for their freedom. We ate our bounty and thanked King Neptune! The winds had blown and fallen as we went! Any lull we would look for in new winds and we would chase any breath we could find. Morale was generally sound and never waned in these times. Except for Seb, whose patience, like usual, ran low even in the best of times. His morale seemed constantly tested. This particular day, he kept busy below deck on the navigation system.

"Bugger, the satellite's gone!" grumbled Seb.

He picked and played with buttons and frequencies for over an hour. In the end, he lost his patience. As a last resort, he turned to smashing the navigation system with a spanner and his fists.

"What are you doing?" I said, frantically trying to stop him.

"Alex, what the hell! Why did you not get that hash? It's been over four days now and I'm clearly losing it!" He smashed the system again, throwing his spanner at it for good measure. "See?" he yelled, throwing the spanner yet again into the hissing, smashed-up equipment.

The system went dead.

"Who cares about that?" I yelled back at him, referring to his hashish. "How the heck are we going to get there now, you idiot?"

"It's fine, I can do celestial navigation."

"Oh great, what are we now? Exploring the Galapagos with Charles Darwin? Re-enacting *The Iliad* in Greece?" I replied.

"Yeah, something like that," retorted Seb. "Actually, that's a good idea! You're right, we are explorers looking for adventure. Chasing our dreams in the sea!"

"OK, Shakespeare," I muttered.

Seb was not one to harp on about emotions and poetry, so his behaviour was a little worrying. The anger I understood, that was his natural go-to emotion, like nearly every male on the planet. But the weirdness was just… weird. I'm not a psychologist but I did start observing him a little closer. The commotion we had made was loud enough to cause concern and Charlie came down to check on us.

"What's the matter?" she said. "What's happened now?"

"Our highly esteemed captain has just smashed our sat-nav and radio!"

She looked horrified as Seb carried on.

"It was already broken! What do you expect, the boat's been sitting on a dock for months and it's gone to hell!"

"Just like us! Listen here, Seb! You had better bloody well get us to shore safely. Or…" Charlie trailed off.

"Or else what? You'll kill me with a frying pan! Again?" yelled Seb. "You can hit me all you want but you won't kill me because I am immortal!"

Charlie and I looked at each other. We were both thinking that was a strange comment. Observation number two for me.

"Listen to you," said Charlie. "You should just get over yourself and get us back to land without killing us. Please."

"Well, now, thank you, Charlie!" said Seb in a sarcastic tone. "The captain has noted your wishes and agrees with your great idea. Thank you!"

Seb was now referring to himself in the third person. Observation number three and my alarm bells were ringing. I thought our captain was sliding down a slippery slope.

Anyway, I'll get back to that growing concern. In the meantime, we had no navigation aids and we all stomped over to Finnbar. He was drunk and sat back, amused by it all. Seb left and soon returned. He was carrying his navigating tools and a map which was flapping about in the wind.

"Listen here, old man! You better get us to this damned treasure, ya hear!" said Seb.

"We shall see, captain," smiled Finnbar. "We shall see."

"Well, what the hell does that mean?" screamed Seb.

At that point, Alonzo came up from below, holding the broken pieces of the battered radio and communication system.

"Aye, aye, aye!" he panicked. "What is this, capitán? What if I need to call my mother?"

"Oh, don't you start, Spaniard, or I'll knife you with your own blades," said Seb calmly but firmly.

We fought for the rest of the day. The mood onboard had changed like the wind. In all honestly, by the end of the day, I think our band of comrades had disintegrated into a squabbling mess. Finnbar was drunk most of the days and nights, he would pass out and then we would wake him up for his watch keep and navigation. Charlie was surprisingly OK; she would help with watch and helm duties but was still distant. She still didn't want to be there, but she got on with it as she had no choice. I was totally infatuated with her, so my judgement was lovingly impaired. The Spaniards were pretty great at cooking for us all, but they stayed mostly down below, cuddling and kissing. And of course, as I mentioned, Seb was grumpy as hell because he hadn't smoked pot for nearly a week. I was beginning to think he might be going into a psychosis of some sort.

But we were past the midway point on the Atlantic journey, jammed up together so, naturally, things were tense at times. Six souls were floating on wood, deep in the middle of an ocean. There really isn't a great deal of space to be found for yourself onboard with a full crew. Anyway, all I wanted was to find this damned treasure. It was niggling at me and starting to tear me up.

When Finnbar was drunk – which was all the time – he could get quite dark. If he drank too much and tipped his equilibrium of booze to blood, he would grow snarly and black as a winter's sea. He had become agitated as the evening merged into the night. When we showed him the broken navigation, he didn't care much, but the drunker he got, he started making more comments to Seb about his stupidity. He was now matching Seb's own demons which grew larger from the darkness in the night. The mood on board was brooding. Finnbar slugged at his bottle and the liquor ran down his chin. He didn't speak but his eyes began to lose focus the more he drank. They stared out towards an abyss. Seb saw he was too drunk for any use and grew angrier.

"Here, get off that!" Seb pushed Finnbar off the helm and took over.

Seb took a flashlight in his hand and began setting up his night-time navigation station. He also took Finn's bottle and took in a big swill of it. He drank it dry and threw the bottle to the floor. Finnbar, staring blankly, couldn't talk but he reached into his jacket, grabbed his pipe and another bottle lying beside him.

There was a cold, silent mood for some time as a black sky took hold of the night. Finnbar closed his eyes and started to hum an old sailing ditty. He then slowly broke out into the words.

"I dreamed a dream the other night
Lowlands, Lowlands away!
I dreamt and saw my own true love
Lowlands, Lowlands away!
I dreamt my love was drowned and dead
Lowlands, Lowlands away!"

"Well, that's a nice little mood lifter," snapped Seb. "Nice, real nice."

"Leave him alone, you bully!" said Charlie. "You're the one who smashed the navigation, you dummy!"

"Dummy?" exclaimed Seb in a mocking tone. "Who are you calling a dummy?"

Charlie and Seb carried on their arguing back and forth. Alonzo and Mariposa came up to see the commotion. They were worried too, as we all were starting to get. They joined in to help and defend Charlie as did I. Seb was being a right beast. He started picking on Alonzo, which he had done ever since he'd come on board.

And then Finnbar gave out a mighty drunken roar, silencing everyone.

"ARGHHHH!" he cried in anguish.

We all looked and stopped our bickering.

"OK, OK," he paused, puffing away on his pipe. "So, you want to know if these diamonds and riches are really there?"

"Yeah, might be helpful," I said. "It might give us something like hope."

"Yeah?" He groaned. "Yeah, well, hope won't help, boy. Just leads to damnation. Now gather 'round all of yees and listen up."

We all sat down snug and grumpy in the cockpit. Finn, nearly slurring his words by now, carried on with inebriated gusto.

"Well." He swayed, holding up his fat, large fingers. "I will need to tell the story first. As to why and how it all began. But I tell ya! It ain't pretty. Because she is a dangerous tale my friends, oh yes, indeed."

Finnbar drank more and more as he smoked his pipe. He spat with a foreboding menace I hadn't seen from him before.

COSTA RICA, 1966

We flew into Antigua from London. It was the middle of summer there and it was so bleedin' hot, every little creature trying to bite a chunk out of us. There was a good crew of men, five of us, and we all whinged about the heat. I remember being so angry that day, not 'cause of the heat, but because I'd had a fight with my father. It was the last one we had. He knew what I was up to. No good, of course, and he hated it. He made it very clear. Even in his drunken fog, which was often and just like mine. The acorn didn't fall far from the tree, I guess.

"Finnbar! You go down that path and no good will come from it," he would warn while beating me. He was religious, so could justify a beating as it came from the hands of God. "And to repent you could cleanse your sins," he scoffed.

That's why I left in the first place. I had the steady work he got me on the docksides in Bristol. It was all horrible and backbreaking. It was the job he'd had. But he was too old to do it any more, with a broken back and other ailments both real and imagined. I left o' course, I didn't want to be like him. Broken, busted and relying on the drink. So, I left for the big smog of London, the Eastend way, where the docks lay.

I told him so and we yelled down at each other in the phone box for an age. I kept putting the pennies in just to have another go at him. He never wanted to see me again and told me so.

"Don't you ever come back, unless you want a beating, boy!" he raged.

I never saw him again. He died somewhere in Bristol, angry and lost from the world. It was another regret I used to carry, but time can put place to that. I didn't care after a while; I didn't need atonement or closure. I didn't even know what that stuff was. I just self-medicated and forgave both of us by way of strong liquor.

Looking back, it was a hard thing to deal with when you're just twenty-odd. But he, as was I, we were the sons of a son of a sailor, supposedly good luck in the maritime world we lived in. Ha, bollocks to that! It's not true! No luck came from his demise. And nor to me.

Anyways, he taught me my first knot and took me to sea before I could walk. But, like I said, he drank too much, it was the Scots and Irish blood in him and like me, I've the same blood coursing through me. But I surely did grow to hate him, especially when he was drunk and hit my dear, God-rest-her-soul, beloved mother. But that bastard taught me to sail, to navigate, to be a real sailor. It was no saving grace, but it was something I could use to run away with!

Anyway, back to the job. From Antigua, the boss chartered a small prop plane, just enough for us all to fit. The pilot, who was in on the job, was Mexican or Hispanic in any case. The job was masterminded by the nastiest villain I had ever met. A horrible bloke called Gedha Roslav, a Russian Gypsy Jew. He grew up in the East London ghetto and grew up hard. He was a boxer like most crooks and gangsters back then, and he grew up big and broad. "Big Geddy Rolls" everyone called him. I remember his face to this day. Pockmarks all over it, white hair before his time, slitty eyes, a big nose, and he yelled and spat when he spoke. Especially when he went into a rage, which was often. I'd seen him strangle and beat a man so hard one of his eyes popped out.

He left him there on the London docks; the poor sod was dead the next morning, frozen solid from the winter winds.

Anyway, Geddy was the big man and had jobs for us that he would get thrown by the bigger gangsters around. I worked for him a long time, too long now, thinking back. But it was money and we all liked it.

So, this job he found all by himself, which meant he didn't have to kick back up to the top crooks. He met a guy in London who was South American. An Argentinian, forget his name now. But he told Geddy about a job, he had a cousin or a cousin's cousin working at a bank in Central America. It was the National Bank of Costa Rica.

There wasn't much to Costa Rica except bananas and coffee. And we weren't going there to steal that. But that bank there was where all the politicians, crooked, of course, would stash all their jewellery and stolen gold. It was a holding house for nearly all South and Central America. Even the Africans caught wind of it and took millions from the diamond mines there and would fly them over! If you were a dictator and you stole diamonds from your own national bank for your wife or your mistress, that's where you'd keep your stash. They'd save it for a rainy day and the piles just grew and grew! So, the saying went, that bank was so rich, it used to lend money to God. But we didn't want the gold (they kept that in there too) that they'd stolen from their own countries. The gold was too heavy and this little old bank had another safe big enough to store the gold there too. What we wanted was the diamonds! And rubies! And emeralds!

The place there, the bank, was run by a Chinese man, Chan, I think his name was. His family were poor fishermen from many generations back, but they rose in social rank there and lucky little Chan married into the elite ruling class. But he was more crooked than the dictators and despots that stashed their stolen hordes. He had the rule of the roost all for fifteen per cent of their loot, he took more of course, but Big Geddy knew it was ripe for the picking.

So, this slick Argentinian would get all the shifts the guards and army had down there in the bank and send them by letter to Geddy. Sometimes he'd come to London but mainly he'd send them by royal mail, no less. He sent floor plans and the make of safe in the vault, and the vault build. They were exciting times, I tell ya!

So yes, it was tight security but it wasn't Fort Knox, it was just a backwater banana republic in the jungle somewhere, after all. Big Geddy licked his lips all the way down in the plane ride. The rest of us crew were chomping at the bit too.

There were five of us. Listen up because I'll be saying a lot of names.

Me, of course, I was to drive the getaway boat. We came into Costa Rica on an unmarked private charter, Geddy fronted the money; it was the first time he fronted the money himself from his own gambling den. He was tighter than two coats of paint.

We needed a safecracker of course. The Rat was his name, a London geezer of Geddy's who did most of his jobs. He looked and smelt like a rat, long nose, moles and whiskers on his face, large, bugged eyes and two front teeth that protruded out from his lips. I never got his real name either, but he did his job and he did it well.

We had an explosives guy, that was Baldo, a Yugoslav who was old and crazy. He'd spent his youth bombing Nazis, that's how way back he went. He hardly spoke English and he always referred to himself in the third person. "Baldo goes KaBoom! Baldo can fix! Baldo make happen!" I don't know why he was on the job. We needed to be stealthy and not make a scene, plus he owed Geddy money, a lot. Perhaps he was doing the job for nought to clear his debt.

The last on the job was a Swede called Jackie Hammerstrom, he was our guns and muscle. He did bank jobs with Big Geddy and the Rat. He was a Viking beast, allegedly he was bored one day so he decided to join the French Foreign Legion, then he ran away from them in North Africa because, "They weren't hard enough for him." The mind boggles sometimes at the wickedness of men.

So, anyway, back to the job. The national bank there was on the promenade in the port, so we had a good opportunity to get a quick getaway by sea. We figured too many banana bending guards with rifles would've shot at us on land. That, and none of us knew how to drive on the other side of the road, how stupid is that? So, anyway, that was me, I was the boatman, and I was ready. I carried less weight back then and could sail or drive a stinkpot anywhere on the sea, come hell or high water.

And there we were in the bloody jungle, with the sweat beading down our shirts and faces, as we rolled into the capital, San José. We took the speedboat our Argentinian friend had organised, and we tooled up. We were as ready as we could be. It was the afternoon, so it was siesta time. This was planned, of course. So, half of the bank staff were at home having a snooze, the other half was out to lunch. And the soldiers out the front of the building were slouched down smoking and resting on benches. They were sleeping too, with no one around to tell them off. I sat in the boat, engine running, looking from binoculars as they all entered. I chuckled to myself at how easy it was going to be.

The guys out front didn't last long with Jackie. He knifed one *from behind and broke the neck of the other. He placed them back on the bench, helmets covering their shut eyes. My stomach turned as I waited for what seemed a lifetime for 'em to come out. After what was probably about twenty minutes, they emerged. Chan, who was surprisingly in the bank at the time, was under the arm of Geddy, with a gun held to his head. Geddy gave him a slap and he ran off crying. The other three held sacks in their hands. It was the pay-out. The four of them came rushing back, full of adrenalin. It was crazy to think that was all it took, twenty minutes to change your life. The sacks, full of diamonds, rattled into the boat as Geddy yelled to drive on. I had already started as we sped back to the private landing strip that our plane was sitting on. It was nestled in the jungle, Geddy radioed in to get the plane ready to disembark. It was a beautiful bloody mess!*

I sped along the clear, flat sea as fast as our boat could go. The crew were cheering, Big Geddy was silent but steely-eyed. He told everyone to shut up. We had two more bays to come around and then we would be back to the wooden jetty we left from. We were half a mile out from the shoreline as we came around the last bay.

But then our carefully laid plans came crashing down. Before us were two naval vessels and small patrol boats. But they carried guns big enough to take us out of the water and blow us to smithereens. I was in shallow water and rocks were dotted closer to shore, the boats were practically parked in front of the jetty. We were in a tight fix. We slowed to assess what to do. The captain of one of the vessels stood yelling in Spanish from a megaphone.

"The game's up, boys!" shouted Big Geddy. He swore and cursed his luck. Jackie began to check and reload his guns. Baldo cursed also and started to re-fuse the bombs he'd made on the

plane ride down here. I could see it was not going to end well. My stomach churned its black blood again as I feared the worse. Our crew prepared themselves as I stooped to a halt, just before the guns were in range. We were going down, so I had to think for myself now and I eyed two bags by my feet. I shuffled them ever so carefully behind me and out of sight.

"Are you ready, boys?" yelled Geddy.

I took the throttle right down and, like the thunder of the heavens, a huge roar rang out as one of the large guns on the patrol boat shot a shell above us. It had whistled past us before we could all duck and hide for cover. The other patrol boat started manoeuvring towards us. It was the one with the megaphone and the officer who wouldn't stop yelling.

"OK, boys, stay steady, stay calm, leave this to me," said Geddy, hard-nosed and defiant to the end.

The big man held his hands up as the boat approached. Us others sat low in the boat, hiding our weapons. The men on the patrol boat came aboard. They immediately grabbed Geddy who fought and wrestled them to the ground before he was handcuffed. The Rat was also taken to the ground.

Geddy yelled at the crew and Jackie opened fire. He shot two navy men before the gunner manning the large gun on the patrol vessel opened fire. The gun absolutely annihilated poor old Jackie. Baldo, too, threw his bomb at the boat and he was shot to pieces.

But his bomb did hit, and the large explosion threw everyone off balance and to the floor. The navy guys were trying to put the fire out and that was my moment to grab the two sacks and jump from the stern of the boat. I jumped with all the life I could muster.

The weight of the sacks carried me down deeper. It was what I needed to hide from surface fire. I swam down deeper, so deep

I burst an eardrum. It all felt like slow motion. I swam deeper into the bright blue. I started to swallow water as the great sea walls engulfed me. It was a painful feeling of disorientation and mystery. I panicked as I felt myself drowning. I dropped the bags as I tried to swim to the surface, but I couldn't climb any higher. The water was dense and thick. I was swallowing the deep sea and it took me down lower into its bowels.

And then the blackness of death took me in his arms until it all felt over.

And then... then, that's when it happened.

NORTH ATLANTIC OCEAN, 2001

I opened my eyes and saw Finnbar had stopped frozen, his face wracked with anguish.

"Finn? Finnbar, are you OK?" I asked.

"Arghhhh." He gave out a soft gurgled tone, drunk and broken. "No," he whispered softly.

We were all wide-eyed with jaws hanging low to the floor, listening to his old tale. Alonzo jumped up and gave him a pat on the shoulder.

"Old friend, if you do not want to continue it is OK, we can save it for tomorrow. Get some rest, Finnbar," he said in a consoling tone.

Mariposa also jumped up and gave him a mighty hug. It seemed the touch from her that snapped him back to life. He took a swig, reloaded his pipe and continued.

COSTA RICA, 1966

I was dying, drowning, indeed I was dead but then I saw the light and the dear moment felt ethereal, out of body. But I was saved! I didn't know what it was or where it came from, and you can call it what you want! God's divine intervention, a miracle or a mythic being saving my soul, but I tell you with a hand on my heart, it was a magical creature that took me. It held me and brought me down further into the sea. I was thrown down into the depths of the sea, but I was saved and given back life.

It grew colder the deeper we went, and I knew I was dying, or dead already. But euphoria and ecstasy had come over me. I thought this was the last gasp of my life. The precious joy of existence, taken and ripped from me! I savoured the last breath of existence. But this thing, this holy, mysterious creature grabbed me. It took my mouth and blew the breath of life back into me. Air filled my lungs and I held on to my last salvation. It was euphoric, I was lost, and I let myself go, I felt myself being carried away. As we came to the surface, I coughed and vomited all over myself, but I realised I had survived.

I looked around and realised we had swum underwater to the next bay, far away from the danger. All the way she'd touch my mouth and give me air to let me carry on and survive. Life never felt so magical and precious. I gathered myself, rinsed my eyes of salty water and cried. And then I saw her. It was a magical, womanly being, so beautiful and wild. She was like a mermaid! I swear to Neptune and all the earthly creatures of this world, I was actually saved by a mermaid! She had legs but she could swim underwater for days on end. I cried with wonder.

Amongst the jungle and the rugged shore, she dragged me to these golden sands and took me to an old fishing shack. I sat in there, wet and exhausted. She was a glorious woman, with flowing black hair and skin so pale and pure. Her eyes were a glowing turquoise green and blue colour, like the Pacific Ocean. I was dazed in unbelievable awe! Shock most likely also, I guess.

She held me by the head as I slumped into the sandy floor in the shack, soaked to the bone. She saw I was bleeding from the back of my head, I must've picked up some shrapnel from the patrol boat's explosion.

I was pulled and dragged to get up. I was so out of my skull, I followed her instructions to the jungle's edge where we lay in the shack, crawling on all four limbs like something prehistoric. My Maria, as I called her, had come to my salvation. I followed her to safety and refuge.

I lay there and slept for what seemed an eternity. When I woke, I was awestruck and, in pain, I watched from the floor, observing my saviour. She lived in this shack, hidden from all outsiders among the thick palms and jungle. But she cared for me, bandaging my busted head and my strained choking lungs. Her kindness saved me from hell and damnation. It was my last bastion.

I was in shock for days. No, for weeks! I had lost everything I had but I was reborn. My mind was racing over the previous events, what had happened and how I had got here. I never saw the others again; two of them had been shot up before I jumped and began swimming for my life. But then it was like I was transported to another world. And I was. Her world.

I lay and slept in her home for weeks as she cooked fish soup and fed me, nursing me back to health. Every week I grew stronger. I couldn't talk to her as she couldn't speak, just make sounds. Well, of course, I tried to talk to her and eventually, we made our own sign language. It was something I'd never felt before and it was nothing short of blissful bewilderment. I lived with her and through time, we held each other and felt our incredible connection. I felt so thankful and humble. I praised her every day. I guess I felt love for the first time, and it grew stronger every minute of the day.

Once I had gained back my full strength, I asked her to take me back to where I thought I had dropped the diamonds. We searched and searched for days. She took me down to the depths of the sea. The luminous colours and light felt out of this mortal world. We swam and looked out for each other for days until we found the sacks. I screamed with joy. That night we made a meal back at her glorious shack and we fell in love.

I had never had anyone care for me like that and her love saved me. All the pain I had given myself in life. All the bad deeds I had done vanished in her arms. I felt the greatest love for her, more superior than anything I had ever felt before. I decided there and then that I would never leave her side. My Maria let me melt in her arms. I sang her songs, and she hummed as we fell asleep in each other's arms, our bodies tangled up on the dirt floor, straw blankets and pillows for our bed. On hot nights, I would walk to the shore and bring back buckets of the salty sea and wipe her down. She could breathe on land and sea all fine, and glowing legs like I said. But I swear she was half human and half this water creature beyond my wildest dreams. I don't how to explain it, perhaps an anomaly of our human evolution!

And so, that night we counted the diamonds, rubies and emeralds and I realised I had enough to build a castle, to live on an island, happy, with not a care in the world for the rest of our lives. I buried the sacks deep in the ground. I took the coordinates from an old map which lay on the shelves of her home. It was an old map the fishermen had used before they left the shack long ago. Now, my Maria lived there and forever I would stay. I kept a few diamonds on me to buy supplies, should we need them. It was like my new currency. But I didn't need a thing, I never actually left that magical place. I never needed to. Except to go fishing or look for berries or fruits in the jungle. We had paradise and I sang hallelujah every day.

And then the greatest curse fell down upon me! One winter's day, I was away fishing. On that particular day, I had walked further to another bay and was gone most of the night. I had nearly fished out our bay, so I ventured off further. It was the biggest mistake of my life. But of course, I didn't know it, I couldn't have foreseen it. The irony was, I'd caught so many fish that day I was so excited and I ran back as fast as I could to show my Maria. I ran through the door to our sweet paradise.

But she was gone!

I thought at first she must've gone swimming and hunting herself as she often did. But the hours grew longer, and I began to panic. On this longest night, I grew a giant knot in my stomach. It was unbearable pain. I searched all night for her. I swam into the sea, calling her name. I searched for days which turned into weeks. I called out her name into the wilds of the sea.

I eventually figured she must've vanished back into the sea; that's what I thought when I was calm, sullen and over my broken heart. I tried to rationalise my pain and lost love. When I wasn't so rational, I flew into panic and rage.

Eventually, as time went by, I figured she probably thought she had done her duty in saving me. She was not of this world *and perhaps she wished to move on. It was hard to understand; I thought she was so happy with me. She was so kind and precious. Naturally, I was deeply heartbroken, devastated and just a shell of a man. That's when my ruin and damnation began.*

I kept searching and searching; it near destroyed me and for days, I lay a wreck after each long day back in our empty home. It was as when she first saved me, like death coming to take me away again. I eventually went into the nearest village, walking miles through the jungle. I bought a boat with my diamonds and travelled for miles, further and further out to sea looking for her. I longed for her presence every night before sleep. I yearned with pain, praying she might return. I saw her in my dreams and when I awoke with an empty space next to me, I would sob. I even prayed to every god on the earth that she might return to me.

Alas, she never came back. She never returned to me. It had been close to a year of searching when I was picked up by the local authorities. I spent some months in jail and was told to leave the country. I bribed the police with the money I had got from exchanging some of the diamonds on the black market there. But I got screwed over, of course, and was exiled. I was never allowed to return. The government threw me out with nothing and extradited me back to England. I spent three years in jail on my return for a crime that no one was found guilty of, except me. Nothing was found, so in my eyes, no one had committed it. But of course, no one had ever found the stolen jewels. I never heard of Big Geddy or the Rat again. I heard they both died in jail there. It was like it all vanished into thin air, like it never happened. Or it all fell into the sea like my dear Maria, never to return.

And so, I came out of prison broken, beaten, and ruined. I had had so much love torn away from me. I was never the same again. And I've been fighting with the devil ever since. My demons get dark now, but the booze and time heal the pain. I try to forget with my rum and whiskey bottles. It helps but when I wake the next day and remember the pain, I do it all over again!

So, is treasure there? Probably long gone by now. It was buried deep; you've seen the coordinates I gave you. Though in truth, I really don't know, and I don't care if it's not. Maybe the sands and winds have shifted in time. Maybe the diamonds have disappeared. Maybe they were dug up long ago. But, as I hold my hand to my heart, I'm not going back for them. I'm going back for her. I'm going back for my dear Maria – blessed be her name – if I only live each broken day to see her again.

ATLANTIC OCEAN 2001

We sat in the darkness. Charlie was crying and Alonzo was crying. He was translating to Mariposa, who was also now crying. I was in sad disbelief. It was a fantastical story. Seb, still on the helm, stood up, rubbing his face with what looked to be great pain.

Alonzo spoke solemnly, "My dear Finnbar, that is such a sweet love story of the greatest kind! We will find her, your beautiful Maria. This is not a curse but a blessing of magical wonder!"

We all went to console Finnbar in his broken spirit. All but Seb, who stared at us in great disbelief.

"You're kidding, right? This is a joke, yes? We're going across the other side of the world, on a stolen boat, with a wanted crew, to look for your old girlfriend of thirty years ago, who happens to be a mermaid? A fish with legs?"

Finnbar looked up at Seb with tears in his eyes, looking ghostly and frail and slowly whispered to him, "Yes, I'm sorry. I swear it's all true! Had I told you, you wouldn't 'ave done it. I mean, to be fair, it's an outlandish story. But when we find her, it will all make sense to you, captain!"

"Yeah, you don't say. Are the diamonds there, Finn?" said Seb in a terse tone.

"I don't know," replied Finnbar who then began to break down and cry again, though this time, uncontrollably.

Charlie, Alonzo and Mariposa continued giving him massive

hugs and consoling his poor, wretched soul. I then looked at Seb, who was now whispering to himself. He kept repeating and repeating his words, growing louder with each repetition.

"This is not happening. I'm going to kill him. This is not happening. I'm going to kill him."

I could see the anger growing in his fists. I had been here many times before with Seb, so I readied myself for the human volcano. Seb instantly took a lunge at Finnbar.

"I'M GOING TO KILL HIM!"

I jumped up to block Seb's force. He pushed me away with ease, knocking me down.

"WHERE'S THE TREASURE, FINN?"

I quickly jumped up again to try and hold Seb back from Finnbar. I knew this rage well. Seb had Finnbar by the neck and began strangling him, tighter and tighter. The other three all jumped up with shock and yelled obscenities at Seb, trying to pull him away. Alonzo, Charlie and I attempted to hold Seb down. He was now in a full psychotic rage.

"ARGHHHHH!" he screamed at the top of his lungs.

"Why did I ever think I could trust this guy?" said Seb loudly, talking to himself whilst still pinning Finn down.

We managed to get Seb off Finnbar as he spat and choked, gasping for air.

"The old man is delusional," he said as he lunged again and tried to wrestle us off him.

Charlie was there and tried to calm him down.

"Seb, please! It's just a story, a nice love story. Don't worry, the treasure will still be there, we'll get it. I'll help you!" she said.

"A mermaid? A mermaid?" questioned Seb, who was trying to calm down.

Charlie sat next to him now as we still lay on top of Seb,

bucking like a bronco. He looked at Finnbar with dark menace.

"How do you know she was a mermaid? You were off your head! In shock! Having delusions!" Seb yelled. "I don't believe a word this drunk has said! Why do you think you saw a mermaid, old man?"

Finnbar, acknowledging the sight, slowly stood up, wobbling heavily as he rose. And once proudly standing straight with all the effort he could muster, he stood tall and solemnly declared.

"Because she had gills!" he cried out. "Underwater fish breathing gills! Right here." His fingers pointed. His fat hands tapped the back of his ears, and, losing his balance, he fell back down and slumped into a heap.

"And I saw them with my own eyes!" he cried from the floor. "I lived with them, I lived with her. She saved me. She saved me, goddammit!"

Finnbar languished on the deck, completely broken.

"Yes, of course! Goddammit indeed!" said Seb, now calm but completely dejected. "I think we've actually blown it!"

I, too, was reeling, so I had to wander off to check the forward sails and take a moment to think. It was the dead of night, and the sea was at its deepest black. I peered down and wondered just how true Finnbar's story was. I think we were all losing touch with reality. It was hard to distinguish fantasy from real life, whatever that was. I peered down into the eerie, murky depths and tried to look for a mermaid to give me a reason to believe Finnbar's story. It was just too sensational to believe. I thought about the ancient tales of sirens the Greeks encountered which had led them to run aground upon desolate shores. I thought about the jolly swags who would sing merry songs of mermaids with magical beauty and foreboding danger. But I thought it just couldn't be true. My rational mind ruled it out as folly. But as I peered into the darkness below, I nearly fell in and gave myself the shivers. I quickly pulled myself away from the depths but kept thinking of the great unknown. Nevertheless, I was overcome with dread as we were crossing the sea shackled to a dream.

And at that moment, I awoke and looked out to the west. The stars ahead were becoming engulfed by darkness. Beyond the horizon, I could see a flash of lightning. My heavy heart filled with more dread. The sky was adrift with abandoned darkness. Looking out deeper, another flash cracked the night sky. I called out to Seb, who had also seen the second flash.

"OK, folks!" he called out. "Strap in, looks like we're heading for a storm."

Everyone looked over to the horizon. As the lightning cracked, you could feel panic and fear overcome us all. Seb rose up and began making ready the vessel for storm conditions. He attempted to calm everyone down, giving them sound and loud reassurances and duties for when the storm was to come. But he only managed to scare the hell out of everyone. I was helping Seb strap down anything loose. As the dark clouds gathered, we all peered out. Seb, now silent, looked to be in his own little bubble. We stood together. Seb walked over and took me to one side, far enough from the others to be out of earshot and then he whispered to me, "Alex, you've got to help me here. I think we really are all doomed." He trembled as he said it.

"Seb, are you OK?"

"No, I'm fine, Alex, but I really think we are all doomed!" he replied. "I've had visions about it."

"Seb, I don't believe you're thinking too straight." I grabbed him to talk some sense into him.

"No, no, it's OK. It's going to be all right because I am immortal, remember? I will save us. Don't you worry," he smiled, manic and dangerous.

My heart filled with even bigger fears and anguish. It was the greatest fear I had ever had in my small life. We were in the middle of a mighty ocean and were heading into a storm. That would have been an acceptable risk but, frighteningly, our captain had fallen off the edge of sanity, so the doom I felt was acceptable but not helpful in calming my nerves.

CHAPTER SEVEN

THE SERPENT'S TONGUE

The lightning grew closer. It cracked and thundered unabated. Some of the strikes broke into two. It was wild nature. The giant strikes looked like a great serpent's tongue, deadly and menacing. The serpent was coming to strike its prey. It was all I could think of. It pulled at my mortal soul. We were all fearful but there was still work to be done, in order to survive. It was bedlam preparing for what was to come. Seb was trying to tune into the VHF radio he had smashed, along with the navigation system. It was useless and he was clearly beginning to fray at the edges as he tried to gauge the breadth of the storm with his naked, crazy eyes.

As the swell of the waves grew bigger, so did their roar. The sound was hypnotic and precise. I started counting; two big waves rolled into two and then three small ones. On repeat, it came again. Two then three, two then three and the pattern was so hypnotic. As we drew nearer, the sound of the small ones vanished. Just the large crashes of water and energy remained. The swell was growing, and the noise was almost melodic if it wasn't so harrowing. The sea seemed endless, the motion swaying. I stared out into the darkness. No dent of light could be made upon it. No wind could ever erode the mighty walls of water which rose from the great seas. The water's force was unmatched and fearsome. I stood forward, watching as the sheets of rain came down horizontally like an army marching into battle.

The rain came first as the dark heavens opened, the sound deafening the ocean. Seb was yelling but I couldn't hear what he was saying. I was fixated on the ocean's power. It was vast, this now terrible and immeasurable beauty. Along with the storm that had now engulfed us from above, the ocean too was now hunting for its prey.

"Get back here, Alex," Charlie was screaming from the cockpit.

I awoke and got back to the cockpit. Charlie had the flashlight on the chart. She was desperately trying to keep our course plotted. The chart was folded into a tiny square and covered in cooking film plastic. She was crouched down, trying to keep the heavy rain off it. Seb now wrestled with the helm as, to make matters worse, the autopilot had failed. Under instruction, Alonzo and Mariposa had scurried down below. They were told to strap themselves into their bunks. Finnbar, being the old salt that he was, said he was going to take a nap and ride it out. He too went below deck, wrapped in a blanket over his wet weather gear.

The first big wave cracked on the bowsprit and sprayed a small typhoon onto us. The storm had arrived in all its immense and horrifying glory. Lines of waves came rushing over us, one after the other. It was like a giant sea monster oblivious to us and to the small amount of time we had on this planet. This monster would outlive us all.

"Strap these onto you," yelled Seb.

Lines and clips were tied onto our spray jackets which connected us to our vessel. The fear of going overboard was real. Our beautiful schooner rolled and listed as Seb ripped her back, anticipating the next wave. Up she rose on the face of a wave, and down she crashed into the ocean on the back of it. We rolled and pitched for what seemed like a great amount of time, it felt endless. Seb managed this precariously until the lightning and thunder were over us. We looked up in fear and, like the dagger of Damocles, it swung above us like a pendulum, waiting for our guilty party.

"Hold on," Seb yelled.

The boat's shackles and lines cracked and erupted. Her giant masts creaked and cracked at every moment. The old oak was busting open in the elements. The huge winds flew through us with vengeance. Seb was riding the waves, getting the feel for the motion and timing. He screamed out with delight as his adrenalin had fully kicked in. He slugged down and emptied a bottle of whiskey. He threw the bottle overboard with wild eyes and abandon.

"Come and get us!" he yelled.

I'm not religious at all. In fact, I detest any institution that would summon a god, not of this earth, to confine a person to abstract laws, practises and theories. But I can tell you, I prayed hard that night. Sow the wind and reap the whirlwind. This was karma smashing us into oblivion. I prayed out of pure fear of dying and not knowing what was on the other side. So yes, I concluded my theory was right as I prayed to God, any god that would hear me. Religion was the last bastion of the damned. And I had become one of them. Meanwhile, Seb continued his battle against mighty Neptune with great force.

"YOU'VE GOT NOTHING! NOTHING, YOU HEAR?" he was screaming with white, cold, knuckled fists in the air.

I envied his bravery, but I also knew how questionable his sanity was. He was steering the ship as best as he could, despite his madness.

"Seb, stop yelling at the storm, would you? I think you're

going crazy!"

"Shut up, Alex. I'm having a fight with old Neptune, and I think I'm winning!"

And then right on cue, as if King Poseidon himself was listening and had angrily thrown his trident, a blinding flash of light cracked through the boat. The forward mast became a lightning rod, hitting us like the serpent's tongue. An almighty roar of thunder was instantaneous. The speed of light and sound were in harmony and the giant force cracked the mast. As a huge wave came over us, the mast snapped right off. The old oak keeled over and broke its rigging, now completely unshackled.

"LOOK OUT!" yelled Charlie, with great fear in her eyes.

Charlie ducked, as did I. The mast flew off down our port side. Its rigging whipped past and nearly took Seb's head off like a killer would use a garrotte. Though part of the rigging did clip his cheek and made a large, deep gash. Seb screamed in anger but carried on as blood came gushing out of him, bursting like a water pipe. He didn't realise it until Charlie grabbed him and held his cheek with her hand. He pushed her away.

"GO AWAY! I'M FINE!" he said, touching his cheek and seeing the blood on his hands. His shove to Charlie made her fall back. In the wet, wild weather, she fell and bumped her head. I jumped up to her rescue and cursed Seb.

"What the hell are you doing?" I screamed.

"Take the wheel, Alex. I'm going forward to inspect the damage!" he yelled.

Seb rushed past us and was cupping his hand, collecting the blood still pouring from the gash on his cheek. He started drinking it and licked his blood. That was the moment I knew madness had truly taken hold of him.

"Look what you've done!" I yelled, holding Charlie.

She was knocked out from a blow to her head. Seb took no notice of me, nor her, and carried on up towards the broken mast cursing at the storm.

"Finn, Finn! Get up here!" I screamed chaotically.

I tried to lay Charlie down while I rushed to grab the helm before we came along to another big wave which would've tipped us over. I grabbed the spinning wheel and ripped it back to our compass course. I yelled again to Finnbar, who came slowly bumping above deck.

"You guys OK there?" he asked, still rubbing the sleep from his eyes.

"NO! WE ARE NOT OK!" I yelled. Finnbar looked around the boat that was in near ruins. Charlie was knocked out cold while Seb screamed at the wind.

"Good Lord, what in blazes is going on?" asked Finnbar, quickly swinging into action.

"Grab this!" I yelled.

He quickly took the helm as I went back to Charlie. I yelled out again to Alonzo and Mariposa. The two of them came up on deck, green as trees in their faces. Alonzo was throwing up from seasickness. Mariposa stumbled and helped me tend to Charlie. We took her down below and tucked her up in a bunk, strapped up tightly. Mariposa, God bless her, bumped and fell but managed to treat Charlie's bump and keep a bandage on her. She sat beside her dressing her wound which gushed blood nearly as much as Seb's cheek.

Back above on deck, Alonzo, seeing the wreckage and the large waves hitting us, started throwing up again. Seb continued yelling at the terrible tempest and I felt pure rage and the fight for survival.

"I AM THE STORM! NOT YOU! I AM THE STORM!"

yelled Seb.

Finnbar, oblivious to what had gone on, leaned into me and spoke.

"What's up with Captain Seb? He seems a little odd tonight. Trying to kill me earlier and now this! Is he OK?"

"No, Finn, he's not OK. We need to do something, or he'll kill us all," I screamed over the waves.

The lightning had passed us by now, the waves had subsided momentarily, and the rain had stopped.

"Ah," observed Finn, "we've reached the eye of the storm, the eye of the storm, Master Alex. An eerie place indeed."

"Hmm," I mumbled and could only look at Seb, who was now silent and looking out to the horizon. He came stumbling back, holding his cheek, less animated but still in a strange, mad place.

"This is God's vengeance on us," he said.

"Huh?" quizzed Finnbar.

"For our sins, this is our punishment," he spoke. His eyes were glazed over as he rambled.

And that was all I needed to hear him say. Never had he spoken about God in his life with such reverence. He had officially lost the plot and I needed to get him out of harm's way, for his sake and ours. I grabbed some line and quickly jumped on him, knocking him down. Being bigger than me, he snapped and grabbed me by the throat. He punched me square in the face. His open wound dripped blood down on me. I yelled for help as Finnbar and Alonzo came to my rescue. They pulled him off me as he flexed like a cornered beast.

"Come on, I'll have you all!" he snarled, as we circled him. "Including you, knife boy, and you, old mermaid man."

"Come on now, capitán. Please," pleaded Alonzo, "let us

help you."

"You're all trying to kill me!" screamed Seb, "And you, gypsy boy, are trying to read my mind!" He was now deeply delusional. He then looked at me and screamed out, "Alex! YOU JUDAS!"

And with that maddening scream, he charged at us like a bull. Finnbar rose again and charged back at him, only to be knocked down hard to the floor. The old, salty bank robber slowly bounced back up with the pace of a snail, it was hopeless. And so, Alonzo and I wrestled my old friend to the ground again. Finnbar, surprisingly, charged again and the weight from his belly then landed right on top of Seb's back to weigh him down. Seb screamed like a maniac on a rampage. I managed to tie his hands together behind his back but couldn't pull it tight enough as he bucked like a wild bull and bounced on Finnbar's belly again.

"Not that easy, boys!" smiled Seb as he stood up again. He pulled and ripped and flexed his arms, freeing his hands. Like a rock, he stood right in front of us all, determined to fight and win. And then, a dull thudding noise rang out from behind.

BANG!

He took a knock and fell forward and dropped with a gravitating thud. And there, proudly stood in his place, was Charlie, bandaged up and holding her beloved frying pan. She wore a look of anger mixed with great satisfaction.

I looked at her and smiled, "Again?"

"Well, that little thing sure does come in handy. Bravo, Charlie!" Finnbar quipped too.

As we entered the other side of the storm, we tussled and fought with the mighty waves. With Charlie's help, we had finally managed to tie up Seb and take him down below. Alonzo and I dragged him forward to the boson's locker where we held all our sails. I threw him a blanket and pillow out of sympathy and the duty I owed to him from our history and made sure he was still breathing. I told his motionless lump that I'd get him back to health. But now was not the time. I was exhausted, but we had to get through the rest of the storm.

Back on deck, there was a semblance of normalcy. We carried on hitting the storm and riding the swell. We pushed and pulled until it had died down to a degree that we managed to navigate our way through it. Charlie was back up on deck and plotting our course on the chart. We could still feel the last of the darkness in the air and the deep abyss that we floated on. But, in this arduous hour, we pulled together and persevered. Even Alonzo started to feel better and turn a lesser shade of green. The fresh air on deck was helping and the worst had now passed.

As we sailed on, punching through the waves for the rest of the night, we managed our shifts in twos. Charlie and I worked together and so did Finnbar and Alonzo. We pushed through as best as we could.

"You know Seb has a psychotic disorder," said Charlie, standing next to me, firm and strong as we continued to battle through the waves.

"Yeah, maybe you're right, but he has done this before and pulled through." I lied.

"Uh uh," she continued, "I know I'm right. Paranoia."

"Yeah, quite possibly," I returned.

"Disorganised thinking," she said.

"OK, agree on that one."

"Psychosis."

"Yep, quite possible."

"Delusions."

"Of grandeur. Perhaps. Look, I know, Charlie. I'm pretty worried right now but I'm just glad no one got killed."

It wasn't a normal conversation or something I'd say when I'm getting to know someone. But since everything had gone to hell, nothing seemed real or imagined any more. It was just a blur of reality and mystery which felt surreal. We were clinging on to life and thankfully surviving. We overcame danger and peril. And we were witness to a fantastical tale of Finnbar's. It was exhilarating, unbelievable and exhausting all at once.

As the storm passed and the morning light emerged, my heart lifted and sprang. We had beaten this rage. The mighty sea beast from mother nature's womb had been tamed. The feeling was immense. We had sailed through a force bigger than life itself. I didn't care about the treasure at that moment, and I didn't care much about finding Finn's mermaid. I was just relieved to have survived. I sucked in the sea and salty air and my lungs filled and felt calm again. As we punched on, I could see the light prevail over the darkness. I stood on the bow and watched the sunrise. The last stars were fading behind us and the first glowing rays of the sun began to shine bright and bold. The light was now upon us. Charlie walked up beside me and watched it too.

"Thanks," she said, smiling and exhausted.

I grabbed her hand and said I was happy she was OK. She turned and gave me a big kiss on the cheek, all dirty, salty and crusty. We looked like a pair of drowned rats. But the kiss she'd given me felt magical.

Throughout the night, I swore I would never do this again, the hell we entered and the elements we endured. Hell, I had even prayed.

But for another kiss from her, would I go through all that again? Probably.

CHAPTER EIGHT

PORT OF CALL

After a few days' sailing, we were now a day away from Antigua. It was to be our magical port of call. Our poor old boat was severely battered. She wore battle scars and limped about on the sea, but we still had one good mast and a sail which luffed about in the midday sun with glee. Spirits were high as we were all itching to hit land and kiss it. Mariposa and Alonzo came up from the galley. The rations onboard were sparse. We had lost a lot of stock in the storm and we couldn't fish as we had also lost our rods and lines. Tinned chickpeas were the dish of the day – again. As they came up, Mariposa was speaking away to Alonzo in Spanish; she looked distressed.

"Señor Alex, your friend, the capitán has been banging on the hatch for a long time now," spoke Alonzo. "He is screaming and screaming."

"Leave him there!" said Charlie. "He deserves some pain."

It had been several days after the storm. Seb had been languishing in the locker, still tied up and his psychosis was still very much apparent. We had been checking on him by the hour each day, much like a watch keep on the helm. He was angry as hell and had small fits of rage. Other times, he was more subdued, when he wished to negotiate his freedom. But we all agreed that he was too dangerous to be set free. I went forward to see him. I opened the hatch and looked down at him. He squinted in the bright sun.

"You bloody arse, Alex! This is a bloody mutiny! I'm going to punch you so hard in the face when I get out of here," he croaked out, spitting with anger.

"Seb, that's why I'm not letting you out!" I said, trying to reason with him. "Come on, Seb, you're scaring the hell out of everyone." Sadly, for him, the point was valid.

"A mutiny! I curse this ship, I curse you, I curse Finn, I curse the Gypsies with one of their damned Gypsy curses! And I curse the whole damn lot of you! Now untie me!" he yelled. "NOW!"

"We're heading to Antigua. I'll get you a spliff and untie you there," I said calmly, seeing him tied up. "Once you've calmed down."

"Antigua?" He looked happy and relieved. "That's a good plan. OK, OK, I can deal with that. Just get me out of this."

"I'll be back in an hour. Anything else you need?"

"Yes, get this piss bucket out of here," he said, kicking the soiled bucket away. "And I'm still going to punch you."

He yelled again as I closed the hatch on him, leaving him to rant away in solitary confinement.

"Oh, one more thing, Seb," I said softly. "Take this, please."

"What is it?" he asked, shielding the sun from his eyes.

"Here." I was holding a little pill Charlie had given me, it was a strong sedative she had for sleepless nights. I dropped it down onto his belly.

"Well, what is it? I'm not taking that! It's probably poison. I think everyone on this boat, MY boat, I might add, is trying to kill me," replied Seb.

"Look! No one is trying to kill you, OK? We want to look after you," I argued. "It's a sleeping pill; you need to get some rest."

"Oh, yeah, thanks," said Seb, reflecting. "It's true I haven't slept in a while."

"How long?" I asked.

"Hmm, I don't know, maybe three days," he said.

"What? That's not healthy!"

"Yeah, I guess not. OK, I'll take it," he conceded. "But it better not be cyanide or anything that might make me—"

"What? Go crazy?" I interrupted. "Just take it!"

"Look, I'll only take it if you let me out," he said.

"OK, deal!" I answered. "In fact, you better take two, open your mouth."

Seb was languishing in the anchor locker among old sails and lines. He had bottles of water we dropped down to him. His hands were wrapped and held to his stomach and his legs were also tightly bound. He looked like a half-embalmed mummy. He opened his mouth wide open and tried to speak with it open.

"OK, throw it in!" he spat. At least, that's what I think he was saying.

I took another pill out and threw it down to him. It flew down, hitting his tooth and thankfully fell onto his tongue.

"And the other one please?" I suggested politely

"OK, but you let me out after, yes?" he questioned, still mistrustful and paranoid.

I answered 'yes' and watched him wriggle the pill on his stomach into his hands. He bent his head down to his hands in a way that looked nothing but uncomfortable. But he did it and gave me a self-satisfactory smile.

"OK, I'll let you out but just a bit later, like when we get to Antigua," I said grinning.

"ALEX!" he screamed. "I'M GOING TO KILL YOU!"

I came up on deck with an evil smile and saw everyone was

worried, except Finnbar. He was fine and had probably seen this type of thing many times before.

"Ah," he smiled. "We really are between the devil and the deep blue sea."

Yes, indeed, we were faced with two dangerous alternatives but the deep blue sea, we had suffered and come out the other side relatively unscathed. I would take that over a mentally disturbed Seb; he was a danger when sane.

'THE MAN WHO HAS EXPERIENCED SHIPWRECK SHUDDERS EVEN AT A CALM SEA' – OVID

Thankfully, we didn't experience a shipwreck, but it felt close to it. It was a combination of fear and angst. But I just know we had all come of age very quickly in that storm. Except for Finnbar, of course, he was old enough to not really care; he had seen wild seas many times before. He only truly cared about finding his one and only true love. The hidden diamond treasure, to him, was non-existent now.

Antigua was approaching and Finnbar warned us to keep our wits about us. This place always reminded me of gunpowder and wooden legs. It was full of skulduggery, old and new. We were fast approaching Saint John's, the capital, and our excitement grew by the minute. Alonzo seemed the happiest.

"Oh, my man, my God!" he screamed with utter joy. "I'm going to get myself and my darling the biggest steak they have in the town. I don't care if it's cooked or not, it can run off my plate and I'll chase it with my knife," he raved with excitement.

"I just can't wait to get off this boat full of lunatics," said Charlie, then she paused. "Except you, Finn, and you, Mariposa and Alonzo." Then she looked at me and rolled her sweet blue eyes. "Oh, and I guess you, Alex."

We were heading to the small shipyard in the port. During

the storm, we had lost just about everything, including our sanity. All our communications, sails and rigging were smashed to pieces. It was going to be a wreck of an arrival. Of course, I was worried. Even in this balmy buccaneer town, there were authorities that might not take too kindly to us and, of course, the boat was still stolen. So, we made a plan to pack our bags and be ready to jump ship. It was our plan B which was fast becoming our plan A.

Coming into the harbour, we could feel and smell the beauty of civilization. We were hobbled and broken but that was an afterthought to our safe haven. Immediately, we drew looks from pretty much everyone. We must have looked like Captain Bligh returning from the Pacific, that was a mutiny also, incidentally. But all I can say is that we weren't looking pretty.

"Steady now, people," said Finnbar, standing by Charlie, who proudly steered us in.

"I didn't know you could sail," I commented stupidly.

"Hah," she laughed. "Well, we've been sailing for the last two weeks together but you must have been too drunk to realise."

"Yeah, sorry," I replied.

"My dad was a tugboat driver on the Albert docks! So, yes, I can steer a ship all right!" she smiled.

Our saving grace was our engine, which was surprisingly still running. We putted in, bobbing up and down. Though we were busted up, we felt euphoric.

We headed straight towards the shipyard. Unsurprisingly, the port authorities came over to us. We put on a good show. We told them we needed immediate medical attention for Seb. I looked down the hatch and saw he was completely out of it as he was sedated, heavily. I dragged him up with Alonzo's help. Seb's cheek was not healing well, and the wound was starting to seep and turn a yellowish colour. He looked pretty much like a mental patient. His eyes were glazed, and drool ran out of his mouth. We knew what was at stake, but he didn't wake up, he was so out of it, but he needed to play along. Being alert and not manically yelling would help. Sadly, however, he was the real deal of comatose, and I felt bad for giving him that extra sedative. I think he was totally ablaze with head fog. However, he did manage to stick an elbow, really hard and true, right into my rib cage. I turned to him in pain, and he smiled back like a drooling fool.

"Where are your ship's papers?" the two Caribbean officers asked.

"We lost them in the storm," pleaded Finnbar. "We lost everything! Look at us! We need refuge and rest, then we can sort out what happened."

On seeing our plight and the state of Seb, the two men were happy to assist. It was a clemency we wouldn't have received in France or Spain. They helped us off with our belongings and organised transportation. I loved this place as my nerves quickly disappeared. However, it was true that we needed medical attention, even though we were thieves and vagabonds. We were completely overwhelmed with fatigue and relief. Alonzo kissed the ground like the Pope does when he arrives in a new land. He jumped and landed on the dock, screaming and dancing. Mariposa cried and kissed Alonzo and joined him in his dance of joy. We all felt elation, but exhaustion came over us like the giant waves we had previously encountered. What a sight for sore eyes we were.

Two little golf carts came driving up and the men in them took Seb and me to an ambulance station on the port. The hospital also sent an ambulance that was en route. The other cart dropped the rest of our motley bunch to the end of the port, where civilisation lay. Charlie gave me the name and address of where they were heading; we would rendezvous there later. I thanked the port authorities as they left us, holding Seb upright on the bench we sat at. Seb gave out a big groan.

"Ahhhh, get me a joint would ya?" His speech was slurred but he was painfully coming to his senses.

Conveniently, a Rastafarian man came past with a large cloud of smoke engulfing him. We stopped him and, taking pity on us, he gave us his joint and a bag of rolled-up ones from his stash. Seb smiled and drooled some more as he grabbed it from our new friend and couldn't take in enough of the smoke into his lungs. He gave out a huge sigh of relief. We sat there for a while, waiting for the ambulance. Things in the Caribbean were a lot slower than anywhere else in the world. Well, not slower, just more laid back.

"OHHHH, that's so good!" he exhaled.

"Seb, I don't think it's a good idea, you staying in the hospital," I suggested.

Seb took out another joint and started it up like a puffing chimney. I think the sedatives were wearing off and he was coming back to himself, ever so slightly.

"Yeah." He paused and blew out the smoke. "If we get nicked, we'll never get to that treasure." He had stopped slurring and was calm.

"How's your face, anyway?" I asked.

"It's fine, just a light scratch," he said, now stoned. "This helps."

He took another puff and was in deep contemplation.

"Gee, I went a bit crazy, hey?" he said sheepishly.

"Ah, yeah, just a bit," I said, smiling. "You've got a few apologies to make too."

"Oh God," he moaned, rolling his eyes and holding his head in shame.

It was good to have him back. As the sirens from the ambulance came down the road, we gave each other a discerning look. We knew what we had to do and began to casually slink off from the bench.

It was stupid to leave but the best idea we could think of in our situation. It was only a matter of time before we would get clipped and found out. We had to keep moving, adapt and overcome. The paperwork we would have had to fill out could have trapped us. Hell, I didn't even know if we had our passports on us. I couldn't find mine.

And besides, we knew a guy we could see, a good guy in this line of work. He'd be able to get us to Costa Rica and let us continue our unknown quest under the radar. He was a Caribbean local, of course, and had contacts all over the islands. We met him a long time ago in Zanzibar, where we had worked for him. His name was Chollo. He ended up in Eastern Africa many years ago and the three of us had quickly bonded over cricket and rum. Well, not Seb; he hated cricket, but he loved rum. We ran everything we could get our hands on and smuggled it for him. He had a bar on an island there, along with boats, contacts and depots. He was what you would call a big fish. And he was big in stature, like a larger-than-life Caribbean Buddha. Chollo was a legend! We spent on and off five years down there and the three of us would always be helping each other out of jams and tricky situations.

Plus, Chollo would have more smoke – the spiritual kind – than Seb needed, as well as proper medicine. The marijuana was, of course, all Seb wanted to get himself back on his feet and to get back to the business of treasure hunting. I have to say, it seemed to be effective.

The ambulance was coming down the road, siren blaring. As it passed, we quickly turned another corner and jumped into a taxi. The man driving us was jolly and blasting reggae.

"Yah mon! Where you guys going? Downtown? Da beaches?" he asked merrily.

"Chollo's Bar!" said Seb, with no time for small talk.

I added, "Please."

"Oh," said the taxi driver, wiping the smile off his face. "OK, to Mr Chollo it is!" And we sped off.

The drive was about forty minutes. We drove through plantations of sugarcane and bananas. We went off-road and bumped along a dirt track. Seb, now with his senses, held his cheek in pain on every bump. I was hoping Chollo might have something to help that was fast-acting, morphine or something of the sort.

We pushed on through the jungle and finally arrived. We were on a small little beach which sat below a large wooden colonial homestead that protruded out of the jungle and palms. We jumped out of the taxi, and I pulled out one of the wads of cash Alonzo had given us. The taxi driver took a note and quickly drove away, spraying sand and dirt in my face. Seb was already making his way up the steps from the beach and I quickly followed.

Now, this was a place, Chollo's Bar. There wasn't a white person in sight and there weren't any American tourists. At our entrance, the whole place stopped and looked us up and down. Death stares came from all directions. It was apparent that it was the "locals hang out," a place full to the brim with gangsters, yardies, drug dealers, hookers, strippers and every bit of riff-raff the island had to offer. The music was loud, heavy with base, and the girls danced and shook in a catatonic spasm. The smell of marijuana was overpowering. We walked past a huge guy smoking an insanely large joint and Seb stopped in his tracks.

"Hey dude, do you mind if I take a puff on that?" he enquired.

The monstrous-looking local with thick dreadlocks was a little taken back by Seb's forwardness and, with a pungent attitude, proceeded to lower his sunglasses below his eyes to look us up and down.

"Yo, white Honky! You can puff on this!" he said and lifted his shirt, brandishing a pistol in his belt.

Seb, in no mood to kick-off, acknowledged the weapon but didn't flinch. I held his arm in case he wanted to strike out. He was still volatile given his mental condition, but the self-anaesthetizing did help his calmness.

Then, suddenly, from the other side of the bar, deep in the corner of the room, a man yelled. A huge, fat guy who I knew could be the one and only. It was Chollo, bigger than a grizzly bear. He berated the local Rasta gangster, who froze.

"SEBASTIAN! MR. ALEX! MY BOYS!" yelled Chollo, smiling. He stood up with arms wide open. He held the biggest smile I had seen for weeks. "What a wonderful surprise, mon!"

Seb couldn't resist and grabbed the guy's joint from his mouth and took a huge drag on it. He blew the smoke into the guy's face and said to him, "You should be careful and not blow your balls off with that thing in there. Not safe!" He walked away smiling.

It was good to see he was coming back to his usual demeanour and sanity, if you could call it that. We got to Chollo's table, where he was holding court with his entourage. He had put on a few more pounds and was dripping in gold chains and medallions.

"Hi, Chollo. Been a long time," I said with genuine happiness.

"Good to see you, my friends. Here, come sit, come," he beamed as he pushed two of his boys out the way to make room for us.

We sat down and Seb practically slumped down in the chair. The effects of his smoke were working but his cheek was pretty bad. Chollo looked at him with bright, piercing-red bloodshot, happy eyes.

"SEBASTIAN! Look at you." He looked at him intensely, concerned.

"Long story," said Seb, barely mustering the effort to lift his head.

I, too, looked at Seb closely. He had turned yellow. I think he was carrying a pretty serious infection by now. He looked like walking jaundice. But time was running short, so we cut right to the chase.

"Chollo, we need help!" I said.

"Sure, my friends. What do you need, mon?" he beamed happily.

"A boat," said Seb, "We need a boat, a fast one."

"Uh-uh," I shook my head. "A plane. We need a plane, Chollo."

"Huh?" Seb looked at me in disbelief.

"Yeah, I'm never sailing again. And I'm certainly NEVER sailing with YOU again! Besides, it will take too long," I said tersely.

Seb shrugged. "O, we need a plane, Chollo, a fast one."

Chollo laughed and slapped us both on the shoulder. Seb grimaced from the slap and took a joint from one of Chollo's cronies who passed it to him. He coughed and smiled. He was trying to get back to normal and wore a brave face.

"OK, boys. Anything for you guys! But for a price, of course." He laughed again with his big Buddha laugh. "My special Chollo price."

"Great," we both said in unison.

"When do you need it?" he asked.

"Now," said Seb, deadpan.

Chollo laughed again, "Oh boy, you guys are crazy, haven't changed a bit, mon."

"Tonight is fine, Chollo," I said.

"OK, so where are you going?"

"Costa Rica."

"Costa Rica, hmm, that might cost a little more!" said Chollo, negotiating.

I quickly replied, "It's one thousand, five hundred and fifty-nine miles in the air from here. That's three hours and forty minutes, no returns needed." I hesitated. "Well, maybe a return if we get in a jam. But we'll pay you that on an if-and-when basis," I added.

"Ah, Mr Alex, always the smart one." He then looked a little more serious, fishing for information. "And what are you guys doing in Costa Rica? Some dirty little business? Need some help from Chollo?"

"Uh-uh, we're fine thanks," snapped Seb, in pain.

"Yeah, we are fine, just going on a little fishing trip. We'll just happily pay you and be on our way," I said, pulling out the wad of euros.

Chollo looked down at the money and named his price. "Good boys, very good. Three thousand, then."

"Make it two, there's only three of us going and just a small plane is fine."

"OK, two and a half! Chollo's final price, my driver will take you from here," he fired back.

"OK, deal, but we have to go back to Saint John's. We need to collect our other guy."

It was so and our business was concluded. We needed Finnbar as he had the coordinates on him and obviously, it was his stash of treasure, despite his disinterest in it now and whether what he had said was actually true, any of it. But the deal was done. We shook hands, embraced and started to go on our way. Then I remembered.

"Oh, Chollo, we need something for this. Got any medicine?" I said, looking at Seb, who was turning another shade of yellow.

"Follow me," he said, smiling, and took us through the bar and into a back room. We followed him into what was his office, which looked more like a VIP room in a nightclub. But from his drawer, he pulled out a large bag of cocaine.

"Here, rub this on your gums, and take some for the plane journey." He handed us the whole bag. It was about five kilos, wrapped and taped in plastic.

"That's all you have?" I shrugged and pleaded. "Really?"

Chollo laughed his big belly laugh.

"It's better than morphine! Why? What would you prefer? A little paracetamol?" he laughed.

I truly didn't like that stuff. Yes, half the world was on it, well, those that could afford it. But it turned people into blabbering fools. And we never smuggled it. It was just too dangerous. Seb, of course, seeing it, his eyes lit up. He took it from the desk, split the bag open and grabbed a huge handful. He smothered it all over his lips and his mouth until he foamed with white powder.

"Thanks, Chollo," said Seb, spitting out foam.

"Oh, Sebastian!" laughed Chollo. "Where did you come from? The wild jungle and seas?"

As we left, Chollo threw a bag of marijuana at Seb and laughed again.

"Good luck, boys!" he smiled.

We hugged again and thanked him profusely. It was really great to have a contact like him, he was more of an old friend, really. At least some people were good in this wretched business of ours, but that's another story.

Chollo's driver sped us back to the port. It was his personal car and it just happened to be a very unsubtle bright green Hummer. God help us, and like I said before, I didn't even believe in him, or it, or whatever you wanted to call this higher being of the universe we worked, moved and lived in. But it was a miracle seeing Chollo again. So, thank you for the small mercies, whoever you are. Even if this cosmic order was in the form of a heavily armoured bright green Hummer!

The return back was quick as we headed back to the address Charlie had given me. It was a hotel bar just off the port. The afternoon was fading and the town was bustling with tourists and locals alike having sundowners. We walked in, trying to be calm, cool and collected. But looking at the state of Seb and rolling up in our truck, I figured we were doomed once more. The four of them, Finn, Charlie, Alonzo and Mariposa were sitting down to a huge, sumptuous meal and chatting away. Alonzo had his huge steak and attacked it like it was his last meal on earth. When they saw us, they froze as Seb strutted by, up on his feet again, untied and larger than life. He began to talk ferociously fast. He was high but he needed to make amends.

"Hi, guys. I'm back. Look, I'm really sorry about before. Charlie, I'm so sorry, especially for what happened in the storm, it wasn't me. I was a fool. I was going crazy. Please, forgive me?" he rambled. "And Alonzo and Finn, I'm sorry. I didn't really want to kill you. That's just my manner, just me being stupid, joking around you know. I'm really sorry."

Alonzo smiled and took a bow in his chair. "It's OK with me, Capitán."

Finnbar spoke and interrupted Alonzo's bow, "Well, there are some beasts out there that take your hooks and hopes. You did both. But alas, the captain's back!"

"Yeah, I'm really, really so sorry to you especially, Finnbar." He was begging for forgiveness in his own special way, which was comical.

"Uh, hello?" said Charlie. "What about my extra apology? You nearly killed me, you ass!"

"Yeah, really sorry about that one," he replied. "Just jokes, hey?"

"Seb, you've got the backbone of a damned jellyfish!"

"Yeah, OK. I'll take that. I'm sorry. To you all! But look, I've made it up to you. We've made it up to you." He was looking at me as he spoke. "We've got a plane, Finn! Alex and I are going to take you. We can still find these diamonds, and we'll still take you to find your missing fish girl!"

"Fish?" Charlie spoke up, demanding attention. "She's not a fish. She's the love of his life! And she's a woman AND a mermaid! AND we're all going to help him find her."

Seb carried on, "OK, ladyfish, whatever. We'll find her, no problem. I'm fully on board on this." Then, he paused and, looking totally puzzled, he responded, "Hey, what? You guys want to come?"

Finnbar stepped in and spoke, "Yes, indeed, that's right! We've been talking, gentlemen, and Charlie, Alonzo and Mariposa would all like to join us on our quest. They've come this far, haven't they?"

"Seriously?" I said, surprised, looking at Charlie. I had been truly struck by cupid's arrow so I wasn't unhappy in the slightest. In fact, I was over the moon. I was just thinking of a way we would all fit in the plane and not get charged for it. But it would be fitting as the bond we had all formed together over the last month was almost like a rite of passage into a wild cult. It just seemed right that we should all carry on.

"OK, let's go! Get all your things, we leave now," I said excitedly.

Charlie smiled back and that was enough motivation for me.

The sun was setting on this beautiful island, and I told the driver we were ready. We all loaded in, bags were thrown in the back but, as we drove off, Finnbar screamed in a panic.

"Wait! My box! I've left my box on board."

His little iron box, as we knew, had the map with the coordinates so it was vital we had it.

"Oh my God, you crazy old—" said Seb, until he was quickly stopped by Charlie.

"Hey, don't you start again," she snapped back.

"OK, sorry. Right, OK, you're right. Let's go to the boat," said Seb, still talking a mile a minute.

This was not a good situation. Returning to the scene of a crime was never a good idea, particularly in the most ostentatious car on the island.

"Stop the car, I'll go!" I said with faux bravery. I jumped out and as I left, Charlie grabbed my arm, pulling me back and softly spoke.

"Be careful, Alex!" Her deep ocean eyes melted me right there and then, right on the spot. And so, with a little love in my heart, which helped my courage, I was off like a shot, running down the dockside.

Getting back to the old *Siren Sea* gave me the shivers. I stayed in the shadows as the night fell. I could see several port authorities milling around her, so I crept slowly and cautiously. This could end very badly. I took a moment to think, but, strangely, I could only think about the concept of rock bottom.

The thing with hitting rock bottom is when you think you've hit it, you feel a sense of relief. You think to yourself, "Great, things can't get any worse now." That is until you get hit again and fall further through the cracks of life; until your life keeps falling further down, and you keep spinning further out of control. And you feel relief again because you think on repeat: "Yes, I've hit it. Now, I'll be fine." Just then, I had an epiphany that there actually is no rock bottom, just decisions and consequences. It's all in my head, this negative concept. So, after my internal pep talk, I was ready. I finally concluded it was just my mental outlook that needed adapting. I looked up at the boat and I was ready. I just needed to stay positive. I approached the port authorities with confidence.

"Hi, guys. How are you?" I looked at the boat and looked at the men again, shaking their hands.

"Oh great, you've found this vessel. Fantastic. We've been tracking this vessel for some time now."

The three men looked at each other and then at me suspiciously.

I continued, "I'm from the Royal Agricultural Society and we have been led to believe this vessel is carrying a very rare and dangerous wood-eating weevil."

The three men looked at the boat and me again. One of them turned to me and spoke: "What is this?" The others pulled out guns and pointed them two inches away from my face.

"Lock him up!" said the officer. They grabbed me and pulled my arms behind my back. I was freaking out and tried to negotiate again.

"Wait! Wait!" I cried out, struggling with them.

My positive mental attitude could take me only so far. I was screwed and felt a little more rock hitting my ass.

Then from nowhere, on the dockside, our bright green Hummer came racing down and pulled on the brakes hard. It screeched to a halt right beside us. The driver poked his head out of the window and yelled.

"Winston, man! He's with me. He needs to get on board."

The officer looked at me with contempt. I stood there like a fool, looking totally embarrassed and ashamed. But I was saved once more by Chollo.

I spoke up sheepishly, "Ah yeah, sorry. I'm with him."

"Hey, Charles. OK, man," he said to our driver and then yelled at me to hurry up.

Quickly, I jumped on board, grabbed the box and ran past them apologising again. I jumped into the Hummer, thanked Charles for his saving grace and sat in there silent. Speeding off, Seb sitting in the front turned around and smiled as he spoke:

"Nice job, Al, nice job," he smirked.

"Shut up," I said.

Yes, I stand corrected. It's not what you know but who you know. We got to the plane and left the Caribbean.

CHAPTER NINE

THE JUNGLES OF COSTA RICA

Everyone slept hard and deep on the plane, all but Finnbar. I awoke and looked at him staring out to the horizon. It was another early dawn as more brilliant pink sky emerged. But it was a peaceful moment and a smooth flight. All was calm. Yet poor Finnbar wriggled incessantly in his seat. I could see his apprehension and nerves.

"Finn, are you OK?" I whispered.

He looked at me and was lost momentarily for words.

"Hmm, no," he murmured. "No, I'm not all right, Master Alex."

"Huh, I can understand. It must be tough for you," I said, then paused. "But we're finally here, it's what you wanted."

He gave out a long sigh.

"Ahhh this is true, 'tis true indeed, Alex. It's just that I've…" He choked on his words. "I've been chasing this bloody past of mine, but that was another lifetime. I just can't let it go!" he said, coughing and deflated. "I just can't let it go and sometimes I wish I could. Because I feel it will come to nothing."

He carried on, "Hell, I sometimes think it's all just been a waste. I've held this sacred moment I had in my life that lasted for hardly a year. But it's been so dear to me that it's consumed me. It's consumed me trying to get it back. And at other times, it's destroyed me trying to forget it," he said in anguish. "What a waste."

I really felt for him. "That's not true, it's never a waste; if it all fails and you don't find her, you've still got the memories. Beautiful, happy memories are everything. The moment you had you will cherish forever, right?"

"Ah, it's not the same; memories fade. One day, you'll understand, but you're still too young. You get old and you forget, plain and simple. You can hold a memory, but in the end, the memory ends up holding you to ransom and trapping you. And you can't escape them."

"You feel trapped now?" I asked.

"I don't know what I feel now." He spoke with a heavy heart. "I look out at the ocean and think of her. I've sailed thousands of nautical miles because it makes me feel closer to her. But then some years, I've felt it all a waste, an intrusion that I've tried to drown out with liquor."

He sighed with melancholy.

"But it always comes back, and I always reminisce about her. To have that love for someone is the greatest feeling in the world. But then to have it pulled out from under you is the greatest pain and suffering you can ever imagine. Time just never healed me and that's all. It just made it worse."

"It can't be worse than cancer." I tried to offer a consoling gesture.

"Uh, what do you know?" he grumbled.

I looked across to Charlie who was fast asleep. I watched her body rise and fall with each breath. I felt love, I guess, but I wasn't really sure. Who really is? But he was right in that I hadn't lost whatever I had found. I hadn't loved and lost, not like him. So really, I couldn't truly understand. I just listened in and thought it just would be best to be there for him.

"It'll be all right, Finn, we'll search for her. You never know what life will dig up," I said

He laughed. "Huh! Dig up? Life will dig up my bones one day, my boy!"

"Ha! Well, I'll make sure I'm there to place your skull and cross your bones in the right spot," I replied.

We both laughed and he waved me to go away, jesting. I paused a moment before speaking again. "Finn, was she really a mermaid?"

Finnbar dropped his head, wiped a tear and was lost deep in thought.

"I don't even know any more; it was so long ago now I can't really remember the truth. Maybe in my own imagination, I just conjured her up as one. I might never know," he sighed.

Finnbar looked out again to the horizon and gently nodded off. It was a deep moment I was left to process in solitude. The feelings Finnbar carried on him were just too sad to give it too much thought in case I, too, would be tainted with the pain he had carried for so many years.

The plane began to turn and swing towards land as the pilot notified us of our approach. I guess it was time to find out.

The bump onto the tarmac woke everyone. The last favour Chollo had arranged for us was an off-road jeep to be left at the landing strip. He threw some digging tools in the boot for free. That man's tentacles ran far and wide, but it was the last wish he had granted. From now on, we were back on our own. And we knew, given what happened to Finnbar, that we were entering enemy territory. We loaded the jeep and said goodbye to the pilot, who quickly went to refuel. There was a solitary man sleeping by a fuel shack. He slept through our arrival. We drove off before he woke and noticed. It was as stealthy as we could manage.

The drive through the jungle sprinkled with coffee and banana plantations was quiet and peaceful. But the tension was there. We all felt it. Seb was driving, against everyone's wishes. He tried not to speed but it was like watching a child the night before Christmas. I navigated with a road map left in the jeep.

It was an eerie place, still early morning, but not a soul to be seen. Just one gas station we passed, with old Coca Cola and Marlborough cigarette signs out the front. We kept travelling until we met the sea, driving north along the coastline. I turned to see Finnbar already looking deeply out to the water. It was dead calm and the sea's surface was like glass. It was mystical.

Finnbar had given me his map, and I could see we were drawing closer to our own little El Dorado. He spoke up excitedly, eyes still fixated on the sea.

"I recognise this now, we're getting closer," he said, springing to life.

The coast road veered to the right and inland. According to our map coordinates, we needed to keep going straight but there was a large hilltop of dense jungle stopping us. We drove further looking for a track, but nothing appeared.

"We've got to get out and walk," snapped Seb.

It would be several miles, but it was our only option. As the sun rose into the sky, the tropical heat came with it; it would be a tough hike, but it wouldn't stop us. The jeep pulled into the edge of the jungle. We were off the road, covering the jeep up with shrubs and palm trees.

And so the march to riches began. Along with shovels and a pick, there was a machete in the boot. Alonzo jumped at the chance to lead the way. He swished and cut at every leaf and branch in front of us. I was right behind him with a map and compass. Charlie and Mariposa, behind me, carried the shovels.

To the rear was Finnbar, wobbling along, and Seb held up the back, looking behind for any unsuspecting locals which there was little chance of, given the remoteness we found ourselves in. He proudly carried the double-barrel shotgun he had stolen from the boat. Charlie wasn't happy that he had a gun, but Seb was in good spirits and appeared to have his psychosis in check. Finnbar and I kept a close eye on him. We headed up the hill.

"This here jungle is lowland rainforest," said Finnbar.

"It is so pretty," smiled Charlie. "Anything we need to look out for?"

"Yes, bats and pumas!" he laughed. "And frogs."

We all gathered closer together at the mention of big wild cats. It was warm but wet. The vegetation was thick and the tall trees were tightly growing together. Exotic birds and butterflies were everywhere. Alonzo would stop when in reach of a butterfly and try to catch it for Mariposa. She smiled so sweetly at him. We trekked on upwards.

"I just love nature," beamed Charlie as we walked. We were in single file and she was behind me.

"Yeah, besides the pumas," I replied. I spotted a beautiful toucan in the branches above her. I stopped to look at it and looked at Charlie. The sun shone down from above her and broke through the palm trees. Her hair glowed rose gold with the rays shining onto it.

"It's just so beautiful!" she said. "I could sleep under the stars here and just let this place engulf me."

"Yeah, there are malaria filled mosquitoes here," was my lame reply as we carried on walking.

"Urgh! Stop being such a crank, Alex!" she said. "You're a real cynic, you know that!"

"Huh? Not true!"

"Oh yeah, really? Ever been spontaneous? Ever fallen in love?" she asked, as I stood in silence, listening. "Have you ever fallen in love with someone who will never let you go to sleep wondering if you still matter?"

"Ah, no," was my quick, shameful reply.

"See, you're a crank!" she smiled smugly.

"Well, I let you guys come on this trek. That's not cynical. That's being kind, warm and inviting!" I said, digging myself a deeper hole.

"YOU!" said Charlie in a huff. "You didn't decide anything! It was *my* choice to be here, and I get to decide how I want to live and what I want to do with *my* life, thank you!"

"Sorry, I'm just trying to be spontaneous!" My replies were getting worse.

"Spontaneous? That doesn't even make sense!" said Charlie, angrily. "You're so negative with your smart answers! Do you actually like anything?"

The conversation had escalated without me realising but it was a good question. It was the first time that I was lost for words. I stopped in my tracks to think about it as Charlie shoved past me. She gave me a look of contempt. She then stopped and turned, looking fierce and angry.

"Here!" she snapped. "Listen to this."

"Ah, I don't hear anything except squawking birds," I replied.

"OK. And what about this? Can you feel the wind on your arms?" she spoke again, deeply annoyed.

"Yeah, a little I guess," I said.

"Well then, that is it. This is life, being present, just being," said Charlie.

"Yeah, OK," I answered dumbly.

"So, just try and listen and feel the wind on the hair of your arms, and you might just appreciate life and find something you like!"

She turned back and marched off, angry and determined. I froze momentarily.

"I like adventure," I yelled out to no answer. "And cigarettes," I mumbled to myself.

Finnbar walked past me and chuckled.

"Way to go, Al, way to go!" laughed Seb.

Reaching the summit was long and arduous. But from above we could finally assess the lay of the land. To our east was the coastline and beautiful shining sea. It was crystal clear and looked so inviting. I guess this is why Finnbar called our boat the *Siren Sea*; it reminded him of his found love. And knowing what Finnbar told us gave me a bigger sense of mystery and wonder I hadn't felt before.

To the west, we could make out a small village town with a white church steeple. To our north, below our climb, was what we needed. It was the map leading us down to the bay. Finnbar gave an assured nod of confidence. In the distance was a broad outline of what appeared to be his old fish shack. I could just make out bricks and corrugated iron from binoculars and thought that must be it. Finnbar started running with his great hobble down the jungle hill. I took the shovels from the girls as they ran after Finnbar to help him down. The elusive pot of gold at the end of the rainbow had finally come to pass. Seb gave out a wild yell and slapped me on the back. This mad adventure was drawing closer to an end. Finnbar was welling up and slowed his pace, taking his time to come down the rest of the hill. It was clearly emotional for him, and we all carried a little hope for him.

Alonzo and Seb broke through the last of the jungle and

landed on soft pink sand. Finn told us the pink sand was from fish eating the outer reef of pink coral in the bay. They ate so much coral that they would excrete pink. The sand was soft and fine; we all ran down and jumped all over the place. It was a time to rejoice in hope and opportunity.

"There it is!" sighed Finnbar, eyeing his old Shangri-la.

But the old fish shack we saw in the distance was nearly demolished and heavily overgrown with jungle. Only one wall of bricks stood up to father time. The floor, in pretty much its entirety, was covered in dense jungle growth.

As we arrived, Seb and I started looking frantically for the palm tree Finnbar had described. It was the mark of his treasure but there were dozens of them. The girls and Alonzo sat Finnbar down, who was huffing from the hike. He pulled out his pipe and looked out to sea.

"Here!" Seb yelled out. Without waiting for an answer, he broke into a sweat, digging into the sand, deeper and deeper, hitting water and nothing else. Then, he frantically ran to another palm tree.

"Nope," would be the call from Finnbar as he'd look around and see another palm tree dug around it, with sand flayed everywhere.

This back and forth carried on for several hours until Seb lost his patience and demanded Finnbar come up from the rocks at the beach and help find his marker.

"Bloody hell, Finn!" he yelled. "Are you going to come and help?"

"It's got an 'X', the palm tree has an 'X' carved into the trunk. Christ! What else would it be?" said Finnbar, losing his patience.

"Could've told us," moaned Seb.

We searched manically for this 'X'. It had been thirty years of tree growth so the possibility of it still being visible was low. Until Alonzo finally found what looked to be a carved 'X' on a trunk, still pulsating like an ancient scar.

Finnbar nodded and said, "Yep, that's your trunk."

Alonzo shrieked and cried out, "The dog who digs the deepest will find the bones."

And before he had finished, Seb was digging and shovelling like he had been possessed.

"How deep did you bury it, Finn?" cried Seb.

"Deep enough," was Finn's reply, as he surveyed the sea.

I could see he couldn't care less about the diamonds. All he wanted was his love back. At that point, I tried to care for Finnbar, but I was too hell-bent on digging for his diamonds. My moral compass was spinning. I too became possessed as I dug and dug until my hands bled. The hole we made was deep and we hit the water again. We splashed about and threw ourselves into the muddy sand.

And then we hit it. We had actually hit it! A yellow canvas sack started to appear. Seb and I gave out a scream. Everyone but Finnbar came running over.

"It's here! It's here, Finn!" I yelled.

He was despondent, still looking out to sea. Seb pulled out the two sacks, both had deteriorated and split; diamonds came falling out the bottom as Seb threw them up onto the sand. We all screamed and started picking through the wet sand to find them. It was a frenzy of elation. Mariposa gave us her jacket and we folded all the diamonds, rubies and emeralds in it. I held up a glowing ruby to the setting sun. It shone fire-red like the blood sky.

In all the tin-pot jobs we had done, with all the danger we

had put ourselves into over the years, this was the crown jewel. We had done it! All the blood, sweat and tears were finally worth it. I wiped away a tear of joy and went running over to Finnbar. Charlie was already there, hugging him.

"Well, I'll be damned, Master Alex. I really didn't think they'd be there." He gave a wry smile and drifted back to his thoughts.

"I thought Maria might have taken them; I wish she had. It would have been a nice life for her."

Charlie stood and looked out towards the sun and sea. She looked beautiful and so kind. She looked down at Finnbar laying on an old piece of driftwood.

"Finn," she spoke. "Come on, let's go find her."

She took off her shorts and top and headed for the water.

"Come on, Alex." She turned to me.

My heart skipped and I followed her in. Despite my awkwardness in the jungle with her, seeing her, I realised that life didn't get better than this. Seb came running over and gave Finnbar the biggest bear hug anyone could give.

"WOOO HOOO!" He screamed out for joy at Finnbar. "You did it, Finn! You bloody did it! You're gonna be famous! AND RICH!"

The old man gave out a grumpy grunt and began to smoke his pipe. Out in the water, I swam up to Charlie and went in to kiss her. She pushed me away.

"Alex! What are you doing?"

"What? I don't know. I thought it would be OK to," I said, surprised.

"I'm trying to find Maria. And I don't want to kiss you. Don't make it weird." She started calling out her name, both above and under the water.

"Yeah, but you really think we'll find her? Come on, Charlie, if she is actually a mermaid, she's probably been eaten by a shark or something."

It was probably the worst thing I could've said. The disdainful look I received was more frightening than the storm.

"You're an ass!" she said coldly, swimming off.

Of all the greatest mysteries of the world, to me, the greatest of all was a woman's thoughts. I swam back with my tail between my legs. But getting back to shore, I quickly perked up. We had millions of dollars' worth of diamonds to count.

And so, we made a plan. We set up camp, made a fire in the relic of the fish hut and we would hike back in the morning to the jeep. That was Seb and I's plan; the others wanted to stay a few days longer and search for Finnbar's lost love. But I knew his love had vanished with the tide and the sands of time. Nevertheless, it was still something we had to negotiate. The sun was setting and we all, except Finnbar, had a precious magical moment by the fire, telling stories about how we would spend our riches.

As night fell, Alonzo, Seb and I took watch duties until morning. The girls and Finnbar played tarot cards and that cheered Finnbar up immensely. I came back from my watch and sat down to see them smiling and laughing.

"Go on, Mariposa," laughed Finnbar. "Do it again. Deal me again, dear Mariposa."

The beautiful Gypsy princess gathered up the cards and began to shuffle. She began to talk aloud in Spanish to Charlie, who had gathered some basic Spanish and began to interrupt Mariposa's actions.

"Tarot cards are here to give guidance," she spoke and listened carefully to Mariposa. "To the elements that orbit your sphere."

I looked over at the cards, and the pictures were so ornate with gold and dark red trim. The deck was full of brilliant colours and images of people, elements and symbols. Mariposa knocked several times on the deck of cards and went into a type of trance. Her darkened brown eyes turned to ebony. Charlie observed and then continued.

"Mariposa is spreading her energy onto the cards. She is asking her spirit guides to be with her during this reading. She is asking for a clear message that will illuminate the highest of destiny paths we can ask for."

She spread the cards out like a fan and looked deep into Finnbar's eyes, into his soul.

"Choose the cards you are drawn to, Finn," spoke Charlie.

Finnbar smiled and reached over to touch the card he wished for. Mariposa slowly flipped it over. The Sun card was revealed. We all looked on, mesmerised. Mariposa carried on with Charlie, listening intently.

"The Sun, Finn," she spoke. "This is a good card in Tarot, possibly the best. It reflects happiness and contentment. It represents good things and positive outcomes to current struggles."

"Well, strike me down!" laughed Finnbar. "You see, positive outcomes, my dear friends. Looks like we might just be seeing my dear, long-lost love after all!" He smiled and looked out to the black horizon. The sea moved and roared, slow and constant as the waves hit the shore.

"OK, Finn, take another card," said Charlie.

Mariposa stared deep and fierce into him as he slowly chose another.

"The Moon!" said Charlie. She looked to Mariposa, who

paused and did not smile.

"Well?" said Finnbar, looking for an answer.

Mariposa took a deep breath and continued. Charlie interpreted as best she could.

"The Moon card is a card of illusion. It often suggests something that is…" Charlie paused as she listened, "… not as it appears to be! A misunderstanding or a truth you cannot…"

Mariposa paused and showed a sadness which seemed to seep from her pores. She carried on and Charlie resumed.

"… A truth you cannot admit to yourself."

I looked to Finn as his head dropped like a lead balloon. No good would come from this and I was getting taken in by this mysterious ritual myself now.

Mariposa closed her eyes and waved her arms across her face in a slow, fluid movement. Finn looked broken again and spoke.

"What's she doing? What does this mean, this card of illusion? It's not true! It was real! I never dreamt it! It was real, I tell you!" he stammered.

Alonzo then stood up and spoke.

"It is OK, Finnbar. Mariposa is looking into her soul, into her third eye."

I looked up and saw Seb had wandered over, looking out to the jungle but listening in.

"Really?" he said in a mocking tone. "We've just found diamonds worth millions and you guys want to freak yourselves out on some gypsy voodoo?"

"Will you shut up, Seb, and just go away!" yelled Charlie.

"Yeah, I'd be happy to," he replied and wandered a couple of steps away, yet I could tell he was still listening in.

Mariposa suddenly stopped and gave out a long, loud breath.

And continued.

"It's OK, Finn. You have one more card to draw and we gather all these cards together," Charlie spoke softly, "This is not your future, Finn! It's about what might happen and deciphering the messages."

This was beyond my comprehension. I was getting drawn into this mystic game. The fire we had made flickered and shot sparks of crackling wood up to the heavens. I knew the bohemian life was fraught with great love, mystery and danger. But this was testing my sanity. Hell, Seb was right. We needed to leave as fast as we could and go get rich. Unfortunately, it was dark, and we were stuck between the deep blue sea and the jungle.

Everyone had now settled down again. Finnbar composed himself and tapped his final card. Mariposa slowly turned it over and my heart and head filled with dread. The card showed the Grim Reaper, the skeleton messenger in black armour. He was riding his white horse and held aloft his bloodied sickle. Of all the cards, it surely didn't have to be this one. I felt fear and dread which I hadn't experienced since our Atlantic crossing and raging storm.

"The card of Death!" said Charlie in hushed whispers.

"Are you kidding me?" said Seb, perched under a palm tree, peering over at us.

"This is not good," I chimed in.

"I've been cursed!" said Finnbar, all white and ashen.

The two ladies whispered to each other and turned to us. They tried to calm the panic.

"No, Finn. Death doesn't mean death," pleaded Charlie.

Finnbar stared at the fire in silence.

"No, Finn," continued Charlie. "It means the end of one phase of your life and a new beginning."

"She is right, Finn," added Alonzo. "It is the closing of one door and putting the past behind you."

Alonzo then leaned into Mariposa, listening to her, as she continued interpreting the message with sobbing eyes. Alonzo stood up and spoke.

"It is the end to the dark night of your soul, Finnbar. This is good! Trust me. Trust Mariposa. This is really good, Finn!"

"No. This is really bad!" said Seb, now angry and animated. "What the hell do you guys think you're doing? You're scaring the crap out of an old man *and* me. All this bloody gypsy voodoo."

"It's not bloody voodoo," replied Charlie. "It's the universe speaking and it's just an interpretation."

"OK," I interrupted their impending argument and spoke. "No more talk or any shuffling of tarot cards! I mean, hell! Charlie, couldn't you have rigged the pack to deal something better? Nicer? Like the Magician, or the Star? Or even The Lovers card?"

"Oh, well, that would have been nice for you, right, Alex?" replied Charlie, now equally angry and upset.

"I didn't mean it like that. OK, look, I can't deal with this," I said. "Let's just all go to bed; we've got the diamonds. We can look for Finn's mermaid in the morning. Good night."

And with that, we all found separate corners in the camp and kept our thoughts to ourselves.

"Uh, Alex, it's your watch," smiled Seb, as he walked up and handed me the rifle.

"Great! Thanks," I replied sarcastically. I sat down under the palm tree and mumbled obscenities to myself for a good ten minutes until I had calmed down.

The jungle was dark but came alive with sounds. I must've

smoked a million cigarettes that night. I had gotten completely spooked as we all had during the tarot reading and I was anxious about spending all the treasure I had spent already in my head. I didn't want to stay another minute here in this wet place. I prayed for the world to spin faster so to bring the sunlight quicker. I didn't want to have my greatest prize and riches that I had found, and then have it all smashed away and taken from me.

I looked out into the darkness and my paranoia grew. I looked at the bag of diamonds under Seb's sleeping head. I stared at it just to make sure it was still there. Then I turned, darting back into the jungle's darkness surrounding me, looking out for panthers, pythons and any other wild or imaginary beasts. I was going crazy. It was madness that, on reflection now, was the mountain of greed which was growing inside of me. It twisted my thoughts and set me adrift.

I kept thinking about the tarot card reading and Finnbar. Maybe the cards were right, and it was all an illusion. I looked over to Finn, sunken low in the sand and snoring, louder than the jungle. I grew mad at him and thought about his wild, delusional story, some mystical mermaid, as ancient as the sea it came from. I didn't believe it and looked out to the water, angry and unkind. I searched and even cried out her name as Finnbar had done.

I looked and hoped, but saw nothing.

CHAPTER TEN

THE VILLAGE AND THE CIRCUS

As morning came, we packed and argued again. The sea blew a salty air into our camp. It was a holiday paradise, but not even our view and newly found riches could halt our fighting. We fought the entire morning until Seb and I decided to yield. We came to a compromise. We agreed that we would all head to the small village we saw from the hilltop. There, we would ask around and search for Finnbar's Maria. I was certain it wouldn't take long, but I was happy to make the gesture. And from the village, we could plan our exit strategy out of Costa Rica.

We trekked back up the hill. The pace was heady, and we remained alert. We now had our treasure safely in our hands. We held the sacks tight, keeping them protected from anyone who might try to snatch them from us. Our adrenalin drove us onwards.

In the distance, the village church bells rang out. By the time we got back to the jeep, the afternoon sun was scorching the earth and us. We hastily loaded up and drove towards the tolling of the bells. It didn't take long until we found the hillside town. It was three in the afternoon – we counted the church bells. The town looked poor and downtrodden. The smell of old fish in the market was overpowering. Small children, barely in rags, came running out to us, desperate, with arms stretched out and begging hands. They tugged and pulled at our clothes. They wanted money, anything. Some of the children were hawking wooden trinkets. Several of them gathered around Seb, who towered above them. They pulled at him and touched his sack of diamonds. He pushed them away, accidentally knocking one of them to the floor.

"Seb, try not to make a scene and get us killed. I know it's a habit for you," I said.

"Yeah, funny," he said. "Can we just make this quick?"

"It will take as long as it takes," interjected Charlie.

In the town square stood only us and the village children. It felt like a ghost town, but this was normal during siesta time. Then, blowing smoke from the top of the square, a small truck drove around us in the town square. Old Spanish horns blared from a large megaphone strapped down on its roof. The children cheered and ran towards it. A man in the passenger's seat held a microphone and yelled like he was in a bullring. The children cheered and laughed. I asked Alonzo what was going on.

"There is a show this evening," he said. "There is a big fiesta."

"Oh, wonderful," said Finnbar.

"It's a fiesta for the sea," added Alonzo.

A larger crowd gathered, with men and woman opening their shutters to greet the truck. The truck stopped and swung open its back doors. The villagers cheered as several men stood over them and began to throw bread, fish and cakes out to the people.

"We should be going to this," spoke Finnbar with a glint of hope in his eyes. Seb naturally reacted with his usual haste and impatience.

"I'm not staying here for another day. She's a bloody imaginary mermaid, Finn! And if she's as old as you are, then I hate to say it, but she'll be long gone, mate."

"Well, I'm staying. I can feel something in my bones," he

stated stubbornly.

"It's probably your arthritis, Finn," I said

"That's enough, Alex!" demanded Charlie.

It was true, the town had a strange vibration. It pulsated with energy which was deep and insular. It felt like it was cut off from the outside world. In the square, the fountain that was dripping drops of water now burst into life and flowed with gushing water. The people ran towards it and threw flowers and gifts into it with voodoo-like religious fervour. It felt so backward, almost dark, macabre and deeply superstitious. Alonzo carried on.

"The circus is by the sugar cane fields. This evening."

A young boy held out his hands, selling tickets for the show. Charlie took the tickets and gave him some money.

"We can ask around for her there, Finn," she said, ignoring Seb's requests.

"OK, stuff this. I'll be here. Call me when you're done," moaned Seb. He walked off to the local tavern by the square and I went to join him. We sulked in the late afternoon sun, drinking the local sangria and smoking cigars.

After a couple of hours of dreaming about our spent riches, the rest of the team returned and sat on our terrace. No sign had arisen of Finnbar's old lover.

"Can we go now?" yelled Seb, now drunk and obnoxious.

"NO!" said Charlie, firm and determined. "No one could answer us, they didn't know what we were talking about."

"Yes, but one old lady told me," spoke Alonzo, "that all the villagers will be dressed up tonight for the Fiesta. All kinds of fish and sea creatures and monsters will be out. It sounds really fun!"

"NO!" yelled Seb.

The church bells clanged and rang again. And from nowhere,

came chaos. The people of the town burst out from every rundown house, shop and cobblestone path that you could see. They sang and rejoiced for the night's fiesta. They were heading south, towards a bridge and across the river. On the bridge was an array of giant lanterns, glowing in the night. And below, on the river, were thousands of candles, floating on tiny rafts, sailing down the stream with the current. We all got up and stared. It all looked so pretty and mesmerising.

"Come on! Let's go!" said Finn with steely determination.

"This is a bad idea," mumbled Seb. He was drunk but, like us all, felt a magnetic pull towards this beauty. "But I guess we can have a little look." He stood up and clutched his bag tight.

We carried along the river. Floating candles and lanterns led us towards an open field full of lights and fires. In the middle of the field stood a big top tent. Alonzo and Mariposa jumped for joy. The circus had come to town!

It was wild and exciting. Flames and lanterns were hung everywhere. Another, larger crowd had already gathered there and manically greeted us all. The people there had painted faces. It was like the Dia de los Muertos, the Day of the Dead carnival. Shadows came from all directions. The glowing, spinning lanterns swayed in the wind. They threw flashes of light and fire into the crowd.

There were ladies dressed in scales and costumes of the sea. All the children ran wild with faces of all different colours. There were sharks, whales and all types of brightly coloured fish. Seb and I began to feel a little on edge; he held the sack even more tightly.

"Look lively, people," he said.

"You shouldn't have that here, you know," I said to Seb.

"Look, there is no way I am letting this out of sight," he

puffed at me.

Finnbar, now as drunk as me, became agitated and began calling out, "MARIA! MARIA!"

Three women came running to him.

I spoke to him, "Finn, you know there will be no shortage of woman called Maria in a South American town."

"Alex," interrupted Charlie, "leave him be, let us at least try."

"Well, I'm just saying." I was puzzled.

"Stop being a twat and help, would you?" she snapped back.

Charlie was the first among us to get mobbed. We were given monstrous painted faces. I looked at her and thought even when angry, she looked beautiful, probably even more so with her fierce, warrior eyes.

We carried on into the big top. The people inside danced, drank and sang. The night grew dark and we felt as if we were entering some kind of cult. Flames and giant candles burned. Men paraded with old swords stabbed into giant fish on wooden trays. They took them to a huge fire and grilled them, feeding the villagers. Two ladies dressed as beautiful mermaids ran up to Seb, they kissed his cheeks flirtatiously. He was drunk and grabbed them both with wild joy. He still held the bags which I watched like a hawk.

"OK, maybe we can stay for a little while," he said, smiling. "We will all meet back at the entrance in one hour," he continued and then he was away, dragged into the crowd by the mysterious women.

I followed right behind, watching the bags. It always amazed me how good Seb was at snatching defeat from the hands of victory. And so, the fiesta continued, and the people grew more manic and deranged. My worry intensified as Seb handed me the bags.

"Hold these, would ya?" he said.

I was now worried.

I walked back towards Charlie and Finnbar. They were still looking everywhere and yelling out for his love.

"She's here, I know it!" urged Finn desperately.

And then a great symphony of trumpets rang out through the tent. The crowd roared. The trumpet players came walking out and formed a large circle. Other men, large and ominous, pushed people aside, creating a huge ring. The crowd roared louder as the lanterns and flames grew bigger with the growing sounds. Two boys marched into the tent and began playing marching snare drums. They hit in time, snapping hard and fast. The drums rolled and the trumpeters rang out again. We sat back and looked on as the crowds gathered fervour. We found a bench and sat ringside to watch what was to follow. Alonzo and Mariposa ran back and sat down with us. They were dancing and laughing and felt well in their element; a pulsating circus had come to town and ignited their passion.

BOOM! BOOM! BOOM!

From the deepest corner in the big top came a loud bass drum, pounding and thumping. Half of the flames and lanterns were put out and the night's atmosphere grew darker and spooky. A wild gypsy choir of women began to wail, operatic and mysterious. The maddening crowd was hushed.

From the back entrance of the tent, where the drummers had appeared, four large men marched out, carrying a covered box. From the bottom corners, it looked to be a large glass tank full of water. Water was dribbling out of the sides. The box was strapped to wooden poles which the men held on their broad shoulders like an ancient throne. The cover came off and inside the tank was murky water full of seaweed and what looked to be a small creature swimming inside. It was dark and I was drunk, so I had to take a second look. I stood up, and to my astonishment, it was a boy. The people stared in a trance, euphoric and drunk. He swam and swam inside the tank, not even gasping for air. The crowd cheered as the minutes rolled by.

"Get him out!" I yelled.

Charlie stood too and began to march towards the tank. She, too, was mesmerised by what we saw. She moved closer but she was quickly knocked down by one of the ringside guardians.

"What is this madness?" she cried out, as I picked her up, standing up to the thuggish guardians. "Alex, it's true!"

She turned to me in amazement.

A ladder was thrown next to the tank and an old man strode up and stood on the tank. It was enclosed and we both grew anxious with shock. The time went on; the boy continued swimming, for minutes and minutes, without agitation or stopping for air. Not that he could, the tank was full of water. I, too, became engrossed in this strange event. As I looked at Finn, he was smiling and beaming. Totally mesmerised and in total bliss.

"It is true!" I said, whispering to him and Charlie, but, really, I was talking more to myself. I couldn't believe it, but the truth hit me like a thunderbolt.

Deep base drums growled out again. They pounded over the choir and another tank came parading out. This one was much larger, requiring eight men to carry its weight.

The old man on top of the smaller tank held an old megaphone and began to talk. The crowd roared as their messiah stoked them into a frenzy. He yelled in broken Spanish, "MIRAD! MIRAD!"

Alonzo translated, "Behold, behold."

The two tanks now stood side by side. the men holding up the tank were sweating, nearly buckling under its weight. The cover was ripped off to dramatic effect. Inside the large tank, among the sea plants and rocks, was another life form, another human body, still and motionless.

And there she was!

Finnbar stood up, his face white like he'd seen a ghost. He was holding his chest in pain like he was trying to stop a heart attack. It was her!

"MARIA!" He stood up, gasping. He fell to his knees as an old monk would do in a state of ecstasy. He had seen his goddess. His cry was of pure love and adulation.

I looked at Charlie. She was crying such beautiful tears of joy, wiping them away in total awe at what was happening. It was surreal and so intense. The mad crowd began to hum and sing in a low chant. I looked down at the two bags of jewels. The straps were tightly wrapped around my ankles. I freaked out and thought of nothing else but getting out of this voodoo cult. But then I realised what I was bearing witness to. Maria was not a myth or folly in Finnbar's mind, she was real. I looked closely at her, in a trance like everyone else. She swam and glided through the water glowing and glorious. She didn't have fins, she had legs like we had. She didn't have scales like a fish, but she had scars and blemishes all over her. She was pale and almost iridescent underneath the water. Her face had pocks and marks, she was not humanely beautiful, but she carried an aura of magic.

Charlie looked at me and spoke.

"Alex, we have to do something, we need to get her out," she said so sweetly and softly.

I rolled my eyes, knowing that it was the toughest challenge

I faced. The storm seemed a million years ago, another lifetime in fact, and yet I actually wished to be back in it. It was something familiar I could understand. This was something beyond my comprehension. I had seen a real-life mermaid. It wasn't just some exotic curiosity. It was a lifeform, so real and so tender. I felt special knowing that this mystery existed, yet I knew it would mean facing another mountain of trouble.

"Yep, I know," I groaned and began to gather my thoughts. "She's been trapped here all along."

Then, from the murmuring crowd, came Seb, shirt ripped and smiling drunkenly.

"What the hell is this?" he yelled like an old cowboy. "This is the craziest, trippiest fiesta I've ever been to! Al, Al, have you seen this?"

"Yes." I was relieved to see him.

"It's her, Seb. Look!" He was pointing at the larger tank. "NO WAY!" His jaw dropped down to his feet and he began to laugh. "NO WAY! FINN!" he yelled. "Can you believe it? This is the craziest, best day ever!"

I could see it was breaking Finnbar's heart seeing her trapped in that water cage. He stayed motion-struck and just stared at her. Seb looked down at Finnbar and, for once in his life, felt empathy and remorse. We all felt great sorrow for Finnbar's poor old soul.

"We need to get her out!" I turned to Seb.

"OK, let's do it," was his drunken reply, and he began rolling up his sleeves.

"Charlie, can you hold this?" I handed her the bags. I was searching for some trust between us.

"Yeah, sure, how are you going to get her?" she asked.

"Not sure yet," I shrugged. "Alonzo, we'll need you."

"Of course, my friend. Alonzo is here for you," he said,

standing to attention.

"We are going to get his fish," smiled Seb. "We'll do it for ya, Finn."

The three of us stood up and began to walk to the man who shoved Charlie. Alonzo spoke up.

"Wait, I have an idea! Let's start a commotion." He began talking loudly to the people near us. His circus showmanship was shining through.

"Se llevan nuestras almas!" he yelled at them.

Mariposa also began to say the same, frantically.

"Come on, Finn! You're coming with us."

I pulled him up off his knees as Seb introduced himself to the thug.

"Hola," he said, and threw the biggest punch I'd ever seen him throw.

WHACK!

The man dropped like a dirty, wet sack. Alonzo carried on with his chant and the crowd, seeing the man fall to the ground, seemed to snap them out of their trance. They began to erupt. The nearby guardians of the ring ran over and the crowd began to jump on them. It was a great diversion by Alonzo as we headed towards the tanks. I turned to him and asked, "What were you saying back there?"

Alonzo smiled and replied, "They are taking our souls! My grandmother taught me when a dog howls for no reason, expect a death."

I wasn't sure what that old gypsy saying meant, but his chant worked and we ran as fast as we could. The men holding up the tanks were shaking and looking over towards the approaching chaos. They saw us coming.

Seb led the charge, screaming for blood. As we drew closer,

Alonzo took out his knives and threw them at the two front throne bearers. They were both direct hits to the belly and the men fell to the ground. The men behind them panicked and dropped the wooden poles. The tank came crashing down. The heavy glass started cracking and the lid fell off.

"NO!" yelled Finn as he looked at Maria.

She had been swimming aimlessly and then was suddenly awoken with a shake and thud to the ground. Water spilt out in a flood. A wave of violence burst through the tent. Mothers grabbed their children, and men fought and punched in the darkness.

As the flood spread out the tank, Maria, too, had spilt onto the dirt floor, now muddy and sodden. Finnbar lost his limp and ran to reach her. I was running also and kept looking towards Maria, now out of the water. It was surreal, she looked so alien, slimy and frightening.

"Maria!" he yelled out, falling into her arms and grabbing her up from the wet trodden soil. "My darling! My darling! It's me, I'm here!" he yelled with joy above the crazy noise.

Tears fell from his eyes as Maria looked up and immediately recognised him. She grabbed him like it was her last gasp of breath. She was old and frail too, like Finn. She had long, flowing, grey hair down to her knees. Up close, her skin was full of freckles, bumps and wrinkles, but she was radiant. She smiled and clutched him tightly. They embraced and held each other like it was the end of time. My heart melted at the love but was quickly angered at the indignity. I looked back towards Charlie, who I couldn't see. It made me nervous and filled me with adrenaline.

Around us, Seb and Alonzo were wrestling with the thugs. I pulled Finn and Maria up, dragging them away until a new fear rose and gripped us. Three thugs jumped upon Maria and the mighty dark and mysterious messiah, who had stood by observing the brawl, walked slowly towards us. He was holding a large wooden bat. This maniacal circus leader strode up like a prowling lion. He was old with a stringy, balding head. He looked nasty and seemed to seethe with pure venom. His face was full of scabs and pockmarks.

"GET HER BACK!" he screamed in English.

Finnbar froze for the second time of the night. But this time out of fear. "Geddy!" He paused in confusion. "Geddy? Is that you?" he mumbled.

From Finn's description before the storm, I think I felt this villain come to life. But here he was in flesh and bone.

"What?" he enquired "Who knows my name?"

"Geddy! It's me, Finnbar," said Finn. "I don't understand what's going on?"

"Finnbar? Finnbar? Is that you?" His face squinted in disbelief. "I thought you were dead! But yeah, it's me all right. Geddy, your boss. What the hell are you doing here and alive, you dirty river rat scum? I thought you drowned!" he spat, curdling with blood-red rage.

It seemed too much for Finnbar to bear. "But I thought *you* died?" he said, gasping.

So, there he stood, larger than life, Finnbar's old boss, Big Geddy! He looked old and nasty. And still fierce and dangerously cold, like an old school gangster would. He looked down at Finn and bade for blood.

It was the weirdest of nights. I'd seen a mermaid for the first time and with that, Finnbar's ghosts had come back to haunt him. He was a deathly white colour. Geddy grabbed his bat, full of menace, and plunged it into Finnbar's skull. Maria shook and tried to scream. She jumped on top of him, trying to protect him.

I instantly rushed at the old gangster, knocking him over. Big Geddy, still holding his bat, gave me a thump to my back and yelled, spitting and cursing, "I'm going to kill you again, Finnbar!"

From the shadows walked a small, thin, twitching old man. I knew straight away it was the Rat. He held a shotgun to Finnbar's face and was ready to strike the trigger.

"Y'all right there, Finnbar? Been a while, me ol' son!" said the Rat with a thick cockney accent. "Now, don't move or I'll blow yer head off!"

Then, from nowhere, Charlie, still carrying the bag, threw herself at the Rat.

BANG!

The shot went off, hitting Finnbar violently in the arm.

He screamed in pain as blood burst through his skin and jacket. He already had blood dripping heavily from his skull. Amongst the ensuing chaos, the three thugs grabbed Maria and pulled her away from the debris. I slowly rose and received another hit to my head from behind. I felt dazed and fell into the mud. I couldn't move, paralysed on the dirt floor. Time and motion slowed painfully. All I could do was watch Seb and Alonzo getting outnumbered and receive a proper battering. It was horrible.

I winced in pain as my head sunk into the wet dirt. My eyes darted around the tent. I could see the Rat whack Charlie in her stomach with his rifle butt. She keeled over and screamed out. Two more thugs approached and grabbed her also. Geddy looked down at the bags and took them for good measure. All I could manage was a raised arm, weak in pain and disbelief.

"I'll be having those!" he spat. "Good luck, gentlemen."

He laughed, dark and evil, slumbering off with smug satisfaction.

Seb rose once more in seeing the bags being taken away. He screamed in desperation and struggled to break free from the thugs holding him down. He broke free and lunged at Geddy in a rage. The men jumped on him and beat him to the ground again. His face was all bloodied and tears ran down his face.

Geddy strolled over and looked down at him like how a dragon would look over its prey.

"What's in the bag then, ay?" he smiled. Nonchalantly, he peered into one of the sacks and grinned. "Well," he smirked, "this has been an eventful night then, hey, gents?"

Then, for good measure, he took his bat and whacked Seb in the side of his head. He knocked him out cold, and with that, the battle was over. We had lost everything. I had lost everything. And now, I knew what Finnbar was talking about.

CHAPTER ELEVEN

VENGANZA

Waking up to the cold light of day, the sunrise pierced through my broken sleep. I felt so lost and betrayed. I slowly stood up and saw the aftermath of the battle. Blood, bandages and great sorrow. Mariposa was tending to Finnbar. He was coughing furiously but, thankfully, he was alive. Seb came marching towards me, bruised and battered and gave me a great big kick up the backside as I stared around in a stupid haze. He furiously handed me a cup of coffee.

"I told you it was a bad idea! But you never listen, do ya!" he lectured.

If things weren't bad enough, now I was hearing a morally reprehensible sermon from Seb. It made my stomach churn, more than the state of shock my body was already in. He carried on gloriously.

"We could have been in Florida by now, drinking cocktails, and gambling, with women! AND DRINKING COCKTAILS WITH GAMBLING WOMEN! And just generally living it up, you know. We could have been at my favourite…"

"OK, ENOUGH!" I quickly snapped back, with a voice croaking in pain. Unfortunately for me, Seb didn't stop.

"But NOOOO! You wanted to be the hero! Just so some crazy woman might fall in love with you! And you could be in love forever and ever and never be apart and then get married,"

Seb moaned in a high-pitched mocking woman's voice and continued. "And live happily ever after! Awwww, bless!" He was all bandaged up and sulking. "BUT who's the idiot now, huh?"

It made me immediately think of Charlie. I shot up in fear.

"Charlie! Where is she? Where have they taken her?" I panicked.

Alonzo, seeing our commotion, came over to sit with us. He had been talking to some of the local villagers who had stayed to help us. One of them, a gentle old man, was the village mayor. He was thanking Alonzo for his bravery, begging and holding his hands, kissing them profusely.

"She's in the hills, over by the old sugar mill plantation, the boy also. That's where they live, with *him*. It's like a fortress, they tell me. Finnbar, looks like your boss handed you a big double cross, amigo. And the people here don't like him. They call him the Ring Master and the Man-Devil. It is a bad omen, my friends," he said.

It appeared the villagers were tired of the tyranny shadowing them too. This crazy story was growing bigger than I could have imagined.

"Well, they're not wrong. He's the devil all right. And we're going to run through hell to find him. You in, Alonzo?" I raged.

He sat silently, deep in thought as I continued.

"You don't have to. You know that, Alonzo? You've done so much already and you've nothing to gain. But if you do, we'll give you a bigger cut of the diamonds, if we can get them, of course."

"Hey!" glowered Seb. "Hang on now! Stop giving away our bloody diamonds!"

"We need him, he's handy and there could be a million thugs up there with guns," I snapped. "And it was you who got drunk and gave the bags to me."

"OK, OK. Don't remind me again. Look, I don't care much about the women you need to save," Seb blustered on. "And I'm not going to be a part of some local village uprising and revolution. So, I won't be donating all my diamonds to the poor, needy and downtrodden. They are *my* diamonds and I found them, and I only want *my* diamonds back!"

"Seb, they are not yours, they are ours, and right now, I don't care about the bloody diamonds. You can have my share! But we need help getting the girls back," I pleaded. "And to get back your stupid damned diamonds, if you must!"

Seb's green eyes grew with greed, motive and dark joy. His green eyes were bigger than his black heart.

"OK, I will do it. Let's start the revolution, then! We need the numbers. Let's round up the villagers and let's do it properly this time. Those thieves are going to get a schooling in plunder! Let's take 'em down!" proclaimed Seb, with hellfire in his eyes.

Alonzo, the town mayor and all the villagers had now gathered around us. Despite being obnoxious, Seb was ready to rally the troops. "Viva? Viva! Hell, I don't know what to say. Alex, help me out here!"

"What about, viva let's kill them?" I said mockingly.

"Yeah, good one. Viva let's kill them!" he yelled to my astonishment.

"VIVA VENGANZA!" yelled Alonzo, springing up. The villagers gathered and cheered. Alonzo smiled as he began to sharpen his knife and present his speech to us.

"I do not need your diamonds, gentlemen. This is not about material wealth. For this, my friends, is about honour! For neither money, nor the devil can remain in peace. And we are all wanderers on this earth. Our hearts are full of wonder and our souls are deep with dreams. And to take this away is a sin."

"Bravo, Alonzo!" coughed Finnbar. "Carry on, my boy."

Alonzo paused and scratched his head, trying to think of something more to say.

"And as my grandmother used to say…"

"Oh, God," groaned Seb.

"If you stab out the eye of thy neighbour, cut their two fingers off and dip them in honey. Then cook them in lemon curd and present them to his family in a pigeon pie. If they dine on this on a full moon, his eye will sprout again from its socket."

Well, that was random, but Alonzo managed to pull it back together when he concluded, "But we do this now for Finnbar. We do this in his honour. And we do this now for the village people, so warm, so humble. And we do this for all of our Venganza!" He swore and spat onto his blade. He held it up and yelled again, "VENGANZA!"

And the villagers screamed and cheered.

That was Spanish, of course, for vengeance. And all I thought about was the sweet revenge and retribution that was coming to those crooks. It would not be easy. They had money and muscle. But we had enough heart to carry us through, or so I believed.

I also kept thinking and puzzling about how Geddy and the Rat had managed to get away unscathed from the heist way back then and stay in Costa Rica— let alone how they had managed to set up a circus. Most likely, it was local corruption and money which pulled the strings of puppets. But I was going to find out, and if it took blood on my hands, I was ready for that.

However, I really felt deeply for Finnbar at this point. I didn't care about the diamonds, I truly didn't. I had lost them anyway, trying to save Charlie. It tore me up in frustration and failure. Now, I just wanted to save Charlie and get Maria back to Finnbar. It was my burning desire.

"Alex!" Finnbar was groaning and coughing out. "Alex!"

The old sea dog, bless his heart, was slumped over in a heap. I moved towards him to tell him our plan. He looked so frail and weak. Mariposa had bandaged his head and shoulder. He winced in pain at every move he made, even breathing was a painful struggle. A hessian sack and straw pillows were his warmth and comfort. That, and the consoling arms of Mariposa. She nursed his deep wounds as best she could, taking care of this old pirate who we all now truly loved. The village doctor was also there. He whispered to Alonzo in soft tones. I didn't want to listen.

"Finn," I held his hand, which he had stretched out for me to grab, "we are going to get Maria. We will find her. The villagers will guide us up there. We will get her back. I think it's truly amazing you found her again! It's incredible, Finn."

"Aye, indeed, it is, Alex," winced Finnbar. "We found her again," he uttered as loudly as he could manage, patting my hand.

"It was meant to be, Finn. We will bring her back to you. Don't worry."

"Ah, Alex, look at me!" he sighed. "I shall not see her again."

"That's not true," I argued. "You'll be fine, Finn. The doctor's here. He'll get you some help and medicine and you'll be OK again."

"Ah boy, you're too kind, and a terrible liar," he laughed. "And if I don't pull through, I shall die a happy man. Because she came back to me, Alex! I saw her and she saw me again. I felt that warm glow again." He paused. "I can be happy with just that."

"Oh, Finn, stop being so dramatic," I gripped his hand so

tightly and looked away. I couldn't bear looking into his sad glazed eyes. I started welling up.

It was a horrid thought. That a loved one's journey in life might be coming to an end. Finnbar knew I was broken up and could see me suppressing the tears in my eyes. I didn't want to cry. It just wasn't the time. But then when would it be? I asked myself. I choked back the worry and tears.

"It's OK, boy, it's OK." He was now consoling me. "Be brave, Master Alex, be brave."

I wiped a few tears from my eyes and held down the lump in my throat. I didn't want to let it out.

"I just have one last request," whispered Finn.

"Sure, Finn, anything? But you're not dead, you know!" I said with a raised voice.

"Take me back to my home, my spiritual home, where the treasure was. And where *my* treasure was. Where Maria found me, where she saved me. Take me back, dear Alex, to the place I fell in love. That's where I want to die. Take me to my salvation."

A dying old man's request is hard to refuse. I would have happily done it, but I didn't want to waste a minute thinking about what might be happening to Charlie and Maria. Seb was nagging away, desperate to get the treasure back. He could not wait and the pressure from everywhere was nearly unbearable.

"Sure, Finn, but you're not going to die, you hear?" I croaked.

And so, we set a plan. Mariposa, with the help of the village doctor and some of the other locals, took the jeep and drove Finnbar back to the coast. They had supplies and medical provisions and would look after him. I felt confident he would be all right. He moaned and groaned as we lifted him into the truck. We bid him farewell, and I promised him I would return with his love. I felt hope but also great, raging anger. This spurred me on. I didn't want to admit it, but the harsh reality was that we were clutching at straws.

The remaining villagers were ready to fight and sang our praises. The revolution was underway. We stocked ourselves up with their hunting rifles and machetes. After some supper, which the villagers insisted on us having despite my protests, we loaded up an old pick-up truck and headed towards the hill that lay in the distance. In the back of the truck, we strategized and planned how we would execute the revolution. Aggression and rage raced through my blood. I wanted nothing more than to destroy the evil that hung from the hills above us. It was time for a reckoning and with each mile, I grew more and more enraged.

Alonzo yelled from the cabin, "It is another couple of minutes, we need to break off into the forest jungle and go by foot so as not to be seen."

"No! I'm going right through the front door and gonna blast everyone!" blustered Seb.

"No, no!" protested Alonzo. "The patient thief is as a tree whose root runs deep as he waits for the sweet fruit."

"Right, can you just stop it with the stupid bloody gypsy proverbs? You're starting to do my head in... AGAIN!"

Seb stood to review our new battlefield and then continued.

"OK, then, here's my new plan. We go in and blast the hell out of these little cretins. We burst inside and grab the girls and the diamonds. The diamonds first, of course," he said quickly, pumped full of enthusiasm.

I rolled my eyes. "Ah, no, that's what we did last time, and it didn't work out so well. That's why we're here now, you big moose. I agree with Alonzo, we need to go in stealthily."

"I agree with Alex," said Alonzo. "We need to creep in and

slit their throats, one by one by one."

A little too graphic but it was our only sensible option.

The lights of the large plantation estate grew closer. We diverted towards the depths of the jungle, switched off the lights and parked the truck. The villagers would guide us up to the old sugar mill mansion, but many did not want to enter. They were still fearful of this devil. I tried to get Alonzo to explain about the necessary bloodshed in any revolution, but these poor people had now lost the will to fight. Only two of the young men among them were willing and joined us. So, the five of us loaded up and set foot towards the battle.

The jungle pulsated, glowing green and fresh in the darkness. We walked in silence and my rage was overcome by fear. I could only think how literally dangerous love was, as I gripped my shotgun.

One of the young villagers, Pablo was his name, was our guide and point man. He stopped and crouched; trouble was looming. Seb, right behind him, turned back to us. He held his clenched fist high in the air. We stopped and could see the silhouettes of two guards.

Then, like a Spanish ninja, Alonzo raced up to them, crept behind one of them and sliced his throat. Then, instantly, he flung his knife into the other guard's belly. The guard gave a scream and Alonzo quickly took out one more knife from his belt. He held the guard's mouth and stabbed him in the heart. We all quickly followed to see the mess and observed for retaliations.

I turned to Alonzo and softly spoke, "Gee, you're good with those."

"Sí, I know," he smiled. "They are bastardos."

We moved on towards the large mansion. Another two guards stood on steps leading towards two huge wooden doors.

At that point, Seb stood up and said, "Screw this creeping around, let's go, boys!"

He ran towards them screaming and fired his shotgun, hitting one in the belly. The other took aim but Alonzo again flung his knife into the man's throat. He fell and screamed in pain. Seb ran past him and whacked him in the head with his rifle butt on the grand stairs where he lay.

He then charged like a cannonball towards the doors and used the full force of his body to break them down. It was a disaster; he fell back from the charge, cracking his head on the giant oak. Like fools, we had followed him and stared in shock as he lay on the balcony floor. I yelled at him to get up. One of the young villagers helped Seb up and once he rose, his adrenaline kicked in, and, again, he charged towards a window and threw himself in. He smashed the window glass as he flew into the house. We quickly followed behind him in a panic.

Inside, the lights were dimmed on a large, ornate chandelier. Above us rambled a double staircase to the first floor. Several men came running out of the hallway there and began to shoot down from the stairwell. One of them looked to be the Rat. That was a good sign. We were getting closer. Glass splinters and wood flew everywhere.

We found any cover that we could. Seb and I found ourselves behind a brilliant white grand piano.

I grabbed him and yelled through the bullet fire, "You know, you've done some idiotic things in your time, but this one takes the cake!"

A hail of bullets shot into the piano, hitting its tuned strings and exploding notes.

"Oh yeah, how so?" Seb retorted while sticking his shotgun up to fire back.

"You can't even get through a front door. You're going to get us killed!" I screamed over the distorting piano notes. "You went crazy on that boat, and I don't think you've come back."

"You know what the problem is with you, Al?" retorted Seb as we both shot at our attackers.

"No, what? Enlighten me because I'd love to hear it," I yelled back.

"You've got no balls!" said Seb angrily. "You think you're so smart but you're not. You've just had vacuum surgery where your nuts have been sucked up into your brain."

Seb and I had had plenty of arguments, fistfights and altercations before, but never during a gunfight. It led me to believe he was right. Perhaps I wasn't that smart after all. Otherwise, I wouldn't have been where I was right then. Still, it was a totally unique and unprecedented moment for us both, and we do all react differently under pressure.

"Oh, yeah?" I retorted. "Well, you're so dumb, if you were an eye surgeon, you'd probably start operating on the asshole. You asshole!"

"Go to hell, would ya?" laughed Seb, still firing randomly over the shot-up piano.

"No! You go to hell!" I yelled, and what came over me was nothing short of stupid instinct and pure bravado.

I jumped up from the battered piano and blasted my shotgun up towards the staircase. One of the thugs keeled over, from what I could see out of the corner of my eye. I raced over to hide behind a thick bookshelf by the stairs. It was full of thick, leather-bound books. I squatted tightly behind it and prayed the books would protect me. The irony smacked me in the face.

I realised the diversion I had created gave Alonzo and the villagers a chance to take a shot at the staircase thugs. One more thug fell and, quickly peeking behind the bookshelf, I saw the Rat and his last crony pull back and dart down the first-floor hallway.

The shooting had stopped. It was a moment to regroup. The smell of gunpowder hung in the air.

"Al," Seb smiled and slapped me on the back. "I stand corrected. You've got big balls! Good job!"

"Come on, you take that side with Alonzo, I'll go up this one with the boys," I directed. I didn't have time to reflect on killing a man. That time would come later no doubt, but not now.

The large chandelier was shattered with bullets as we stepped up towards it. We arrived at the open doorway. Seb snuck his head around to take a look. He saw nothing and gave the all-clear. We crept down the hall slowly and softly. It seemed like a thousand doors were facing us. We checked each one as we went along. Nerves wrecked; the seconds felt like hours. We came to the last door. It was at the very end of the hall. We all looked at each other and braced ourselves before we entered.

SLAM!

Seb busted in and we all followed. Before we could fire a shot, a loud voice came from the far end of the room. It was dimly lit, but we knew the voice.

"'Allo, boys!" The voice was old and nasty. It was the East-end gangster and Finn's dirty nemesis, Big Geddy Rostov! "Want to play with the big boys now, do ya?" he spat as he stood in all his evil glory. He held a gun to Charlie's head.

I froze and shook in a giant panic. I looked around the large room. It was an opulent entertaining room and at the end was a long, illuminated bar. The Rat was also there, brandishing a shotgun, as were another five cronies. They all were spread across the back of the bar. It was a Mexican stand-off.

"Let her go!" I yelled. "You can keep the diamonds!"

Seb looked at me and rolled his eyes. He mouthed a large "NOOOOO," at me.

"And where's Maria?" I added.

"Maria? Maria? Who the hell is that?" snarled Geddy with his menacing laugh.

"You know who he means. The bloody mermaid!" yelled Seb.

"Ah." Geddy gave another evil snigger. "You mean the magical creature from the deep, my greatest money earner and treasure? No chance, boys! She lines my pockets."

He looked towards the Rat. Behind them was a large black cloth, illuminated from beneath. I hadn't noticed it before as my mind had been focused on getting Charlie out of danger. But my heart pounded a little more when the Rat revealed what was behind the large blanket.

Maria and the young boy from the circus were in the tank. Maria looked radiant as she floated in the huge glass tank. The light inside the tank made her look splendid and so iridescent. She saw us from afar and put her hands on the glass. Her eyes were sad. I wanted to cry at her beauty, but the situation was too dangerous and fragile. And I couldn't really enjoy her sorrowful beauty in captivity.

"Let them go, Geddy!" I called out, tensing my rifle.

"Well, come on, then, come and get them!" he snarled back.

This was the moment when the villains and heroes laid their cards on the table. Where the why's and how's were conveyed, and plans and motivations revealed.

Everyone gripped their weapons, intense and fierce. And so, before our battle, I looked at Geddy and asked the question that burned in me.

"Why?" I spoke directly to him. "Why did you screw Finnbar over?"

"Hah." Geddy welcomed the dialogue, "Why, you ask?"

I stayed silent.

"Because that's what we do. Us old-time crooks get a kick out of it!" he laughed.

"But I thought he worked for you? I thought he was your friend?"

Geddy laughed again like a child. "Hahaha, there ain't no such thing as friends in our game. It's dog-eat-dog. It's throw-the-lambs-to-the-slaughter. It's who's smart enough to outfox the other. And it's kill the weakest and feed off the corpse. It gives you the power and HE WHO HAS THE POWER ALWAYS WINS!" he spat with rage.

"Plus, he was too dumb and trusting," he laughed, spitting with poison.

I was nearly broken listening to him. There in front of me was wickedness in flesh and blood. In my head, I wrestled with this evil. No feelings of guilt did he feel from such a betrayal. It was time to meet his maker, SATAN!

"Charlie!" I yelled. "GET DOWN!"

Charlie, from my call, threw an almighty punch towards Geddy. She managed to knock the gun from his hands. Both sides raced to reach their triggers. The first shots rang out as glass and wood splintered and shattered everywhere. Geddy flew into a rage. He pulled Charlie to the ground as they fell behind the bar.

Gunshots flew everywhere and bullets smashed into the glass tank holding Maria. The glass was so thick no lead penetrated through. But as more gunfire bombarded the glass, the tank began to split and crack. It was a sign that Maria didn't need glass tanks any more.

"Stop hitting the tank," I yelled amongst the gunfire.

Maria swam behind a rock for cover at the onset of bullets.

Seb and Alonzo had managed to hit a couple of their guys. But we were still pinned down behind beaten-up dining tables and chairs. They had more firepower than we had expected. They kept shooting and blasting away at us.

A cry rang out as one of our villagers, Pablo, got shot. He fell in a pool of blood from a shot to the face. His friend screamed out and raced over to him. In doing so, he got shot in the arm. Our new friend was gone, and we all knew it. They had the higher ground from the bar. We had nowhere to go.

"We're like sitting ducks here," yelled Seb in frustration. "Go be a hero again would you, Al?"

As much as I wished I could, the gunfire was too fierce.

"Here, hold this," whispered Alonzo, throwing his gun he had picked up from a dead body towards Seb.

Alonzo pulled out his knives and set off crawling under the dining room tables and debris. Towards the bar of death. We desperately fired as many shots as possible to give him some cover.

Seb, trying to shoot as many rounds as he could, got nailed in the hand. His rifle sprayed off his hand and he screamed out in agony.

"ARGHHHHH!" he cried. "My hand!" He gripped his hand, and I could see a missing stub from his index finger.

"Seb! Seb! Are you OK?" I called out to him.

"Yeah, I hate you. I really bloody hate you right now, but I'm OK," he grimaced in pain.

The gunfire had stopped from the bar. Seb looked at me and put his shot finger up to his mouth. He pressed his bloodied finger to his lips and didn't say a word. He was shaking in pain.

A whisper came from the bar amongst the smoke.

"Geddy, I fink we've got 'em," spoke the Rat, in his East-end cockney tone. Thirty to one hundred years in Costa Rica wouldn't change that.

"The game's up, boys!" laughed Geddy. "We got ya cornered, you've nowhere to go and this is MY GAFFER!"

He blasted a shot into the lights over our heads. Glass and light bulbs burst above us. We got showered in more debris. He gave out a bellowing laugh, enjoying teasing his prey.

"Alex!" screamed Charlie. "Go!" She was being held by one of the thugs, crying in pain and anguish.

I looked across to Seb, seeing if he was able. I hoped he might have an answer. He looked at me in pain, his finger, wrapped in his torn, soiled shirt, was still pouring blood. At least he was alive, for now, but he was out of action. All he could manage was to pull out his last morsel of cocaine. His powdered medicine from Chollo illuminated his eyes. He forced it into his mouth, again spitting foam, but this time with deep red blood dripping down his arm.

Our villagers were out, one dead, one wounded. Seb was hit hard and couldn't shoot. We were finally spent. In our darkest hour, there was no light. No guiding pilot to be seen.

"OK," I croaked out amid the smoke and haze. "We're done. It's over, you win!"

I slowly got up, every part of my body aching in pain. My left hand was held up in surrender, the right still holding the shotgun, barrel down towards the floor. I glanced around and saw Maria's head poking up above the rocks in her tank. Charlie was still raging with her neck clasped in the thug's tight hand. He was squeezing the life from her. I gave a deep breath and realised I had just snatched defeat from the claws of victory too. It was over, my head sank and the life I had wished for fell to the floor. My hands were shaking in fear. Geddy clocked his gun and pointed. And then…

"VENGANZA!"

It was the great Alonzo, who, in my moment of impending doom, I had completely forgotten about. He came flying in from the left of the bar and plunged a knife straight into one of the thug's ribcage. Both the Rat and Geddy and all the remaining thugs turned towards the attack. The Rat blasted a shot at Alonzo, who, in the same instant, flung a knife back at him.

Alonzo actually missed! And for his efforts, he took a bullet in his shoulder. He fell to the floor, but it was enough time for me to take aim at the Rat.

BANG!

A shot fired off, hitting his stomach and he fell to his knees, holding his bloody guts. It was ugly yet it felt so pleasing. Geddy, on the other hand, was full of venom. He threw Charlie to the ground furiously and blasted his gun at Seb and me until his bullets ran out. He and his cronies ran towards us. Seb was overcome and smashed to the ground. And then a moment of pure Hollywood arrived. The cavalry appeared.

From the entrance sprang a dozen villagers. The old mayor was leading the charge. He held aloft an old sword and wore a jacket from what looked to be from the Napoleonic age. It was certainly the most surreal day of my life. OK, maybe the second, after I saw Maria for the first time.

The villagers charged and blasted, managing to overcome Geddy and his henchmen. Geddy was shot numerous times and fell to the floor like an old bull. The village mob jumped on the thugs and beat them hard and furiously. The remaining villagers tended to Pablo and Juan. Those boys who valiantly came with us, I would thank them forever. Poor Pablo had bravely died, the ultimate sacrifice. Juan was battered but thankfully alive.

I dropped my shotgun and ran towards Charlie. She had taken a heavy knock and was bleeding from her forehead. But she was OK. I fell to the floor and gave her a huge embrace.

She spoke in an exhausted voice, "I'm glad you didn't try to shoot that old crook while he was grabbing me."

"Why?" I asked, smiling.

"Because I saw you shoot clay pigeons, and you were terrible. You would've killed me!" She laughed and gave me a big, bloodied kiss.

I pulled her up and we achingly held each other, neither one wanting to let go. I looked around the destroyed dining room.

Alonzo was holding his shot shoulder in great pain. He was being looked after and congratulated. He was in great pain but shone a beaming smile. He was slumped behind the bar, holding what was probably the only bottle of rum that hadn't got shattered and shot in the gunfight. He was looking at Maria and the boy, swigging his rum and cheering.

Maria was now out from the rocks, smiling and fully pressed against the glass tank which was cracked and close to breaking. The boy was laughing at Alonzo's wonderful animation. A wave of joy and exhaustion came over us. It was euphoric and infectious.

Charlie then turned to me and asked where Seb was. I nodded and pointed in his direction. I hobbled over to his lump of a body, wedged between two old dining chairs. A villager was next to him, looking down with tears in his eyes. Seb was bloodied and out cold, eyes closed, and head slumped to one side. I panicked for a second and feared the worse. My hobble sped up as I jumped down to where he lay.

"Seb! Seb!"

There was nothing. Charlie came running over with a look of great worry. The villagers also stopped their celebrating and came over.

"Seb!" I spoke again, with my voice quivering.

I couldn't feel or hear him breathe as my hands were numb and my ears were ringing from all the gunfire.

"Alonzo, or anyone, get me some water, please," I yelled.

Alonzo's nurse came running over from the bar with a giant champagne bucket full of ice and water. He presented me with the bucket. I shook my head.

"Uh-uh, you do it," I said.

The villager threw the water and ice onto Seb's head, the ice smashing his face. He awoke in a shock and sprung up like an old moose would coming out of hibernation.

"What the hell!" he screamed, swaying his head and squinting.

He looked at the villager who had thrown the bucket and snarled. The villager ran behind his friends and we all laughed.

"Welcome back, Seb," I smiled with relief.

"Urgh," he grunted, still waking up. "Where are the diamonds?"

"Look, we did it. We got Charlie back and saved Maria and the boy."

"Yeah, great! Where are the diamonds?" he returned, ignoring my words. "WHERE ARE THE DIAMONDS?" He was in a panic, looking around the room.

"I don't know," I said hopelessly. "But we got the girls back."

"Well, yeah, that's great, like I said. Good for you, Alex," he spat with sarcasm. "Congratulations! Pat yourself on the back but right now, I couldn't give a rat's arse." He grabbed me, almost pleading, "Where are the diamonds?"

Our moment of victory and glorious revolution was cut down, in flames by Seb's envious desires.

"I don't know," I said again, forlornly. "We can find them."

Seb started strutting around like a bull in a china shop, except all the china had already been broken and smashed to smithereens. He strode off behind the bar and looked at Alonzo and Maria. Alonzo shrugged and couldn't give him an answer.

Seb looked down at the Rat and grabbed his jacket shaking him furiously. The Rat was now cold and dead. Seb impolitely dropped him down again.

"Where's that other old bugger?" He strode through the bar. We all watched him swagger along. He arrived at the lump of Big Old Geddy, the nastiest gangster I'd ever met. Seb gave him a kick. A loud cough rang out through the room.

"He's alive!" I cried out and gingerly ran over to see him.

By the time I got there, Seb had his two fists clenching Geddy's coat and was, again, shaking his victim manically.

"Where are they?" he screamed into his face.

Slowly Geddy came to his senses and spat blood into Seb's face, smiling. Geddy, just alive, mustered a violent slap across Seb's face. I felt the hatred return to my soul. I jumped on him with rage and grabbed his face.

"Tell him," I yelled. "Or I swear I'll …"

Geddy cut me off. "Or you'll what? Kill me? Ha!" he laughed. "You'll never find it." He staggered and spat, "Screw you!"

I grabbed his face and he winced in pain but looked at me with darkness, deep into my eyes.

"It's like a disease being nasty, being evil. And you'll get it!"

"Shut up!" I said, trying not to bite.

"Mark my words, you'll get what's comin' to ya! And when it does, I'll be there to see it." He trailed off, grinning and coughing up blood until he choked and stopped.

"Like a disease," he chuckled, and they were his last words.

So, finally, he was dead. This long night for the soul was over.

Seb dropped him down with a thud. He was livid. I was shaken to my core. The villagers were in shock but relieved. The darkness that lay over their land was now at an end. Maria, who was looking through the glass, gave out a deep breath from her lungs. The bubbles covered her smile. She swam around the tank, flipping about with joy. Her webbed feet, which I hadn't noticed before, flapped and splashed through the water. Her tyranny was over.

I looked over to Charlie. She was staring over at Maria in a trance.

"Alex," she whispered. "Look!" She pointed to Maria swimming about. The tank was glowing and sparkling. Seb and I looked at each other and slowly walked over to the tank.

"What?" I said. "What are you looking at?" And then it struck me.

Sparkling amongst the sand and pebbles at the base of the tank were all the diamonds, scattered and shimmering.

Seb looked into the tank and gave out a big yell, "YOU BEAUTY!" as he stumbled over, and climbed up onto the back bar. He jumped straight into the water.

The splash nearly broke the already cracked and fractured glass. Diving into the tank, he gave a wave to Maria and then, through sheer excitement, gave her and the boy a huge, big hug. He dived down, collecting all the diamonds. The villagers gave out an almighty cheer. Charlie and I embraced. Alonzo was jumping for joy with tired tears in his eyes. Seb gave out a scream every time he came up. He handed all the diamonds to us as he rose up to the surface. Eventually, he became breathless and Maria and the boy, seeing what he was doing, began kindly giving him a helping hand.

CHAPTER TWELVE

THE JOURNEY HOME

My thoughts raced to Finnbar. I wanted desperately to see him and tell him the fantastic news as soon as I could. We packed the village trucks with our diamonds, the tank with Maria and some booty from the mansion the villagers had taken the dead and wounded bodies from. The mayor could not stop thanking us. He insisted on a fine banquet, the biggest the village had seen and, on the drive back down the hill, he anointed us. With the sign of the holy cross, he proudly made us Golden Conquistadors of the Village. I took it as a good sign, but I was well and truly finished with my buccaneering smuggler days. And to be fair, I would never experience such a journey quite like the one I'd just had. However, if the mayor was willing to throw us a fine farewell village banquet, then who was I to turn down such an invitation? It was a time to finally rejoice.

The wine cellar back up at the evil mansion had been raided and all of us were well and truly drunk. The drive down the hillside was full of merriment. Yet still, I wanted to get to Finnbar and would pass up all the festivities just to see him. After all, it was his legacy and story, not ours.

Maria and the boy, who were bouncing about in the back of the open truck, would be set free again, after all these years of incarceration. Our plan was to take her back to Finnbar and have them re-ignite their love. I didn't know if the boy was Maria's, maybe even Finnbar's child, but I doubted it, given the age Maria looked. Still, after all this, anything I knew, or thought I knew, went flying out the window.

We would stay there overnight and split our diamond share. Seb had the bags of diamonds tied to his maimed hand. He would not let them slip away again. And so, the race was on to tell of the good news and set sail for the bright future to come. Figuratively speaking. of course.

Arriving at the village, we were greeted by the women, children and the old folk. They cheered and laughed as their heroes came home. The mayor was telling the great tale and legend that had just taken place. I stood up, dazed, and saw the time on the town hall clock was five thirty a.m. Dawn was about to break, and at first light, we would be able to safely navigate our way to Finnbar.

So, after many drinks and celebrations, our motley gang gathered around and readied ourselves. Alonzo was desperate to see Mariposa and Seb began loading up the jeep with our treasure. We bade farewell to the villagers and promised the mayor we would return for the evening's fiesta.

"Let's make this quick," snapped Seb. "We give Finn his share, drop Maria off, and we are done."

"Agree," I said back, realising it had been some time since the two of us had agreed on something.

"So, no more detours, no more gangsters, no more mermaids, no more circus, no more gypsies, no bloody revolutions, no—" Seb barked.

"All right, all right!" I interjected.

Listening to his words, it did seem farfetched. Hence why I had decided to hang up my smuggling boots. And besides, I was kind of hoping things might turn out well between Charlie and me. I wasn't the type to confess my love, but I was willing to stay with her until one of us annoyed the other beyond repair. Ah, romance in the modern age.

I looked at her next to me; she looked a mess, as did we all, but to me, she was more beautiful than ever before. She smiled and whispered a thank you, grabbing my hand. Right there and then, that was enough for me. It was bliss in a bucket of blood.

A couple of villagers drove the truck in front, carrying Maria. They knew another route to Finnbar's hideout, so we followed along. The dirt and mud track had become familiar territory now. We were there in no time and could see the bay as the sun broke out its rays through the clouds. We stopped at the end of the track and both Alonzo and I jumped out running through the jungle.

"Mariposa!" he called out. "Mariposa!"

Despite being shot at, roughly four hours ago, he could still run and had loads of energy. Love will do that, I guess. I followed after him in great pain and, luckily, not a bullet had passed through me. I thanked my gods and, soon enough, we came to the clearing and the old brick, rubble hut.

We looked around and the hut was empty. But on the beach, Finnbar and Mariposa lay on the sand by the water's edge. The local village doctor was sitting on the rocks. The old man Finnbar had blankets on him, and Mariposa was holding him, stroking his white hair. The sun had now come up from the horizon for the day and the sky was a rich streak of pinks and greys.

We arrived at the beach and Mariposa jumped up embracing Alonzo.

She was crying and kept repeating, "Él esta muerto! Él esta muerto!" She was sobbing uncontrollably in Alonzo's arms.

I knew what this meant, and my heart sank. I knelt down to

Finnbar and felt his cold, wet skin. Finnbar was gone. He had slept peacefully through the night and never woke.

Mariposa was telling Alonzo what happened through the night. He was translating for me.

"She tried, Alex, to care for him," he spoke solemnly. "But all he wanted to do was go the water, to be by the water, he wouldn't listen."

I looked to the doctor whose head was sunk into his hands. I felt so sorry for Mariposa and the doctor and thanked them both. I was so sad and started crying. All I could hear between my sobs was the soft lapping of the waves, gentle and constant. And I stared down at the old soul of my dear friend, now gone. I cried again but was now bereft of tears. I just choked and groaned in misery and sadness.

Charlie and Seb were at the hut. They were holding Maria, who looked frail in the morning sun. The young boy followed behind, holding onto Maria's arm. They walked slowly over and knew from the look on our faces what sadness we were all to share.

They arrived and Charlie put her hand on my shoulder. I took it and held it, not wanting to let go. Even Seb managed some condolences.

"Bugger, poor ol' Finn. He was a hell of a guy." He stared down at him, "Cheers, captain, Rogues In Peace."

Maria fell down onto Finnbar's body. She lay next to him and gave out a soft whimper of sound. I could see the gills behind her ears flap and wave as she made the sound. It was sad and haunting. You could see she was lamenting deeply. It was such a bittersweet moment. Finnbar would've been so happy hearing her and being caressed by her loving arms.

And then she gave him a rub of his nose from hers, like what the Maoris and Pacific Islanders do. She quickly looked up at us and pulled at his body. She stared at us with fierce eyes of sadness. Looking out to sea, she began to try and drag his wet, heavy body to the waves. Charlie started helping her.

"She wants to take him with her," she said. "Help us, please."

"A burial at sea," said Seb. "I suppose it's fitting for such an old salt."

"Come on!" I said.

Seb and I grabbed the corners of his wet blankets and carried him into the water like a patient on a stretcher. Slowly marching out to the water, we got out waist-high. His heavy body began to float and dip through the waves. We took the blankets away and Maria took over. She stripped him of his clothes and gently held his torso. I grabbed his feet and gave him a helping push as Maria began to swim further out to sea, holding his body. She called out to the boy on the water's edge, who was splashing around. He ran to her and dived in.

We watched as they swam further away. The sunlight shimmered in the water. Goodbye, old friend, I hope to see you again one day. May your journey to the other side be safe, wherever that may take you.

From the distance, I could see Finnbar's body get heavy and drop below the surface. Maria looked back towards us, she gave a wave and then she dove down below. She was home. We never saw her again.

I turned back and looked at everyone's faces. Sad, exhausted and empty. Seb gave out a big sigh.

"Right, we need to get out of here." He sounded fatigued and sad.

That day, we sat and counted out the diamonds, slowly and deliberately. I kept looking out towards the water. Looking for

Maria and hoping Finn might just reappear.

We were all happy we had something to show for this misadventure but, for me, it was bittersweet. I was sad that Finnbar was lost to us, and I just wanted to go home. But I didn't actually know where that was.

"OK, that's the count," affirmed Seb, packing his rubies and diamonds. "Let's bounce," he smiled.

Alonzo and Mariposa walked down to the sea together, holding hands. They threw a diamond each into the water. Seb looked up bewildered and started yelling.

"What are you doing, you gypsy fools?"

"We are paying the ferryman for Finnbar," Alonzo replied. "We would do the same for you!"

"Ah, no thanks. I can pay my own way thanks, I don't need no saving grace or ferryman," said Seb, looking out to where they had thrown the diamonds, almost tempted enough to dive in for them. He was back to his old cantankerous self again.

"Let it go, Seb," I said. "Stop being so grumpy. We won. And Alonzo saved us!"

"Yeah, you're right," he laughed. "Go for gold, Alonzo! Throw as many as you want."

"So, what are you going to do now anyway?" I asked.

"Not sure," said Seb, then paused. "Get drunk, first. Then maybe take a break in Buenos Aires, I don't know. I met a tango dancer once. She was from there."

Charlie and I looked at each other and shook our heads with laughter.

"What?" protested Seb. "What? Well, what are you two lovebirds going to do then, huh? Make babies?"

"I don't know." I shrugged. "Maybe go on a holiday."

"On land," chimed in Charlie.

"Yeah, in the mountains with no water," I agreed.

"An African desert," smiled Charlie, "in a cave."

It was nice we were complimenting each other's sentences. I smiled back and thought an African desert non-adventure might go down pretty well.

We loaded up the jeep and headed back to the village for the evening fiesta. I was so tired and sad that I didn't feel much up to it, but the villagers made me feel welcome and happy. They revelled in song and dance and wine. The mayor and the townsfolk made speeches all night. One of the speeches, it turned out, was an offer to Alonzo and Mariposa. They had the invitation to take over the circus by the mayor. It would be a village gift and cost them nothing. They obviously jumped at the chance. Alonzo offered to pay the mayor, but he would not accept. It was a magical moment where the universe was kind and generous. We danced and sang and enjoyed the night like it was our first night on earth. All our bright futures were to come.

And finally, late that night, with a little trepidation, I turned to Charlie and said, "So, do you want to go find that café?"

"Hmm, maybe," she said, smiling.

She gave me a big kiss. And I took that as a resounding 'yes'. Well, no, I took it as a resounding 'maybe', but that was plenty enough hope and promise for me.

THE END